GEORGE KNOWS

MINDY MYMUDES

MUSE
I
YOUNG

MuseItUp Publishing
www.museituppublishing.com

George Knows © 2014 by Mindy Mymudes

MuseItUp Publishing
14878 James, Pierrefonds, Quebec, Canada, H9H 1P5

Cover Art © 2013 by Marion Sipe
Edited by Erin Dunbar
Copy edited by Les Tucker
Layout and Book Production by Lea Schizas
Print ISBN: 978-1-77127-543-9
eBook ISBN: 978-1-77127-455-5

To the Tall Dude,
who still helps and supports me.
And, great unpaid kennel help.
Who knew that asking you to help me with my chemistry would
polymerize us?

Acknowledgements

It took a kennel to write this. First, the Breakaway Babes, who have my back, no matter where in the world; thank you Dee Hoosier, Stephanie King, and Enny Oheeal (JK). To my writing mentor and bud, Faith Hunter, who is a great cheerleader and better teacher. George doesn't even mind if she writes about a big cat. The Peeps at The Magical Words site, who taught me so much. Thank you Erin Dunbar and Les Tucker for making George understandable to more than just other dogs. To K-9 Obedience Training Club of Menomonee Falls, Cudahy Kennel Club and Cream City Canines for helping me understand dogs, even if George is a perfect basset hound familiar. Kathie and Michael Giorgio of AllWriters' Workplace & Workshop, helped return my confidence. Kim Weckerly, Sandy Goldsworthy and Kelly Risser gave me invaluable critiques. The Muddy Paws Pack, Chrystal, Cera, and the Freaky Beak, Mandy, for keeping the insanity alive. And Sandy Case, I know you're at the rainbow bridge with your own pack, but spend a bit of time with Charm, Quark, and Joey. Thank you for everything you did for me. You left us all far too young.

Chapter One

"George, what is wrong with you, you stupid dog? Why'd you trip me?"

Humph. She calls me stupid? It wasn't me that stomped on the plant. Way to finish the plant-smooshing process. Guess Auntie Heather isn't going to get her herbs today.

Does that mean no treats?

As Karly's familiar, my job is to help train her to use her skills as a witch. Even with the help of our Auntie Heather, who is very old and experienced in the ways of witches. Karly isn't the easiest Girlpup to teach.

Grrr! Why is my Girlpup so senseless? Bend down, Karly. Bend down, already! It's right there, in front of your nose. If you take another step, you'll squash it and your aunt's going to be upset. Groan. Karly takes the step and squishes the plant we've spent all afternoon looking for. Like most Peeps, Karly walks with her head in the clouds, forgetting there's a whole world at her feet.

Snort. This is about to be fun.

Well, for me, not so much for Karly. I step in front of my Girlpup. She trips over my handsome, low-slung body and lands on her face. The grass is soft enough—she's not hurt. It's just more proof of how silly it is to only have two feet. If she were lower to the ground, the Girlpup wouldn't fall so far. I am built low to the ground, like a sleek motor car. A black, furry car with tan and white trim, that's me. I'm not a racing car, though. It's wrong to waste energy.

Auntie Heather says Karly is a normal Girlpup. She doesn't always pay attention to my lessons. She'll learn...eventually.

Sigh.

Peeps take forever to grow up. She's already too tall for a good basset hound, but short for a Peep. She could use more fur, too, she keeps getting it cut off. It's not very pretty, not like my contrasting patches of light and dark. She looks like a Cavalier King Charles spaniel—her face is too flat, with practically no nose, eyes too round and white, and useless ears on the sides of her head.

At least I get to be with my Girlpup to train her—something I can't do when she's in school.

I shake my magnificent long ears and give her a soft nudge. Karly falls sideways and reveals the smashed remains of the leopard's-bane. Basset hounds are short, but powerful. I bay at the plant, a long "aroo!" Come on, Girlpup—think. Think! You can do it. I've seen it.

Once or twice.

"Isn't that the plant Auntie Heather wants us to get?"

I look into her eyes and show her the picture Auntie Heather left with me. She giggles as she always does when she looks through my eyes. I've seen through hers, too. There are some very strange colors when she pictures something for me. They're very distracting. How do you enjoy smell/tastes, feelings, and sounds if you're tied up with all those colors?

She sighs. "I guess it's lucky you tripped me then." Karly removes her backpack from her shoulder and pulls out pruning shears and a brown paper bag. She snips off a handful of the blooms and tucks them into the bag. The bitter smell/taste fills my nose with cold. There is one last flower on Auntie Heather's list. It's something with dark dots. I concentrate on the image in my mind. It sort of looks like an upside-down mouse. Our aunt calls it jewelweed. I snoofle deeply. Let's see, the plant likes it wet. The smell of wet muck, sweet petals, and… and…rabbit…

Rabbitrabbitrabbit. I've got you. Dinner's in the pot, Karly! Hurryhurryhurryup! "Arrrrooooo!" I look behind me. My short legs are great for keeping me close to smell/taste. My ears scoop it up and feed it into my nose and mouth. Karly, even though her legs are long, is slow. "Arooo!" She's too far behind. I look at the rabbit's trail, blazing warm with new heat. I glance back at Karly and let my legs give way, collapsing with an "oof" on my belly. No way can I get the rabbit and keep an eye on my Girlpup. Auntie Heather would hang me from my ears on the clothesline if I lost her. I don't think it is a meaningless threat, and my ears are plenty long without stretching them.

With a rumble, I wait for my Girlpup to catch up to me. My nose sorts through the smell/tastes without my thinking about it. The long-gone rabbit scent, the trail tasting gray. The doe and her young are too far off to chase. From the edge of the park, car exhaust smell/tastes oily and burned.

What is that? A slithery gassulfurdrysnakecatstink? It's very wrong and doesn't belong here. I lean into the smell/taste and get to my paws. Scratching the ground, the scent boils up—old, musty, damp from spring rains, and frost-raised. Frost makes rocks hatch from underneath the ground, not whatever this is. This is interesting. The thing calls to me.

Where is this thing from? I scrape the ground again, wondering what else is under there.

"George, where are you?" My Girlpup calls. I hear her mumble something about losing her phone, and I'll need to find it.

My hearing is exceptional.

When I need it.

Now is not the time—she's distracting me.

"Agggh! You blockheaded freak. I bet you're chasing a rabbit again. Why aren't you a golden retriever?" Karly has a lot to learn. If she'd just learn to use her nose more, or use mine—that's why we have a mind-link.

I don't understand my Girlpup; the rest of my Pack adores me. Packmom Doreen is always an easy conquest. She saved me when I was a puppy and I fell over my ears, and my legs wouldn't stay under me. She is the most important member of the Pack—she feeds us.

Just not often enough.

Packdad Brian is very well trained and does whatever Packmom Doreen wants. In the last two years, I've become a model of the perfect hunting hound. Karly needs to see me for what I am, and she doesn't.

Yet.

When I prowl in her mind, I see how she pictures me—a clumsy, stupid, wobbly pup. I shouldn't have to prove to her I am the best familiar in the world or that I am brilliant. I shouldn't, but I know I'll have to.

"George!" she shouts through panting. Why is she running? "Where the heck are you?"

Although Karly's scent changed after her twelfth birthday from sweet/milk/FrootLoops to that fake/flower/chemical that she thinks removes her odor, I know it's her. Even if I can't smell her, I can still hear her stumble over the path. Big rocks and trees that scrape the sky get in the way. She needs to get lower to the ground. Now she's sneezing. If only she'd work with me, her allergies would go bye-bye. Whoever heard of an allergic witch-in-training? We can use green magic. But Karly will first have to trust me.

And she doesn't.

Yet.

Maybe when she gets older.

She will.

I continue to scrape my claws into the damp ground, searching for more smell/tastes and listening for my Girlpup. She's panting like it's a hot day. At least she's catching up. I am satisfied she's okay, and dig like a badger with my wonderful big paws and claws, the ideal excavation tools. I wish I was digging up the den of a rabbit. I slow to sniff.

No.

There's no rabbit here.

Something different's calling me.

What the heck is it?

Dirt and roots pile up behind me, and my rear is now higher than my front as I dig. I scrape against rocks and try to push them away. They aren't rocks—too long and thin. I wrap my jaws around one and toss it with a headshake out of the hole. I find another and do the same thing, until there is a pile of buff-colored things that look like bleached driftwood.

I heave myself out of the hole and investigate my find. The thick sticks are hairy with fine roots. I pick one up. It's light for its size, hollow, and about the size of a rawhide bone. It has a round knob on one side and is broken off on the other. I retrieve more pieces from the hole and sit. Maybe they are old branches.

No.

They don't smell/taste like old branches.

Hmmm.

Karly finally shows up, huffing and puffing, out of breath. She needs to get out more. I poke my nose into the pile of things I've dug out. "George, what are you doing? You aren't, um, eating those, are you?"

I look at her like she's crazy. I don't eat wood.

Anymore.

Karly points to the things and counts them. "So what did you find? There are nine of whatever they are." She bends down and touches one. "Weird, they look like someone snapped them in half." My Girlpup takes one of the longer things and rubs off the dirt.

She drops it like it's a pan just out of the oven. I take a sniff; it's not hot. There's something here, though.

Not a good something, either.

"G-G-George, those are bones," Karly's voice breaks as she stutters over my name. I take another sniff. Yeah, they could be bones. What's the problem with that? I lick one. It tastes like dirt. They've been here a long time.

Yup.

That's it.

Just a bunch of animal bones. Maybe a big dog buried them. What's bothering her? The hackles rise on the back of my neck. The not good gassulfurdrysnakecatstink smell/taste spins around my brain like smoke.

Oh.

Oh no.

I hack and cough. I know exactly what kind of bones these are.

I look Karly in the eye and push a picture of a Halloween skeleton. I know she doesn't like it when I go into her head without permission, but this is important. I am not sharing the good stuff, like manure, rotting fish, and dead animals.

"No way. These aren't human bones," she squeaks and backs up.

Nope, she can't ignore these. I pick one up gently between my teeth and carry it to her feet. I carefully place it in front of her toes then shake my muzzle, lips flopping from side to side, trying to get the taste of Peep bone out of my mouth.

Peep bone.

It's awful.

Bassets do *not* eat Peeps' bones. We only chew non-Peep bones. We need our Peeps to hunt for our fresh, meaty bones.

"George, leave it. We need to talk to Aunt Heather about them. She'll know if they're human or not, and what to do if they are." Karly gulps. "If they aren't...I hope they aren't. You've never smelled human bones, so how'd you know?"

Um, I am your familiar. I have magical skills? There's something off about the bones, and a weak scent gets stronger as I inhale.

Blegh.

It's a really bad smell/taste.

I watch as Karly runs to the parking lot where her bike is stashed. Yellow plastic tape wraps piles of rocks and lumber and large trucks with big scoops and flat fronts are parked behind barrels. Auntie Heather told Karly someone called a Developer is going to turn the park into houses. She also said it'll be "over her dead body."

While Karly unlocks her bike, I mouth the blue bandana off my neck and lay it on the ground. I pick up each bone and nose the corners together. Now it's easy for me to carry the bones back to Auntie Heather.

"George! Hurry up, we need to get Auntie Heather's before something happens to the bones."

What will happen?

Will a big bird scoop them up?

No bird is going to like dry old bones.

I'm better than a bird and I don't like the idea they're Peeps bones, either.

Maybe they aren't.

Probably are. I'm never wrong about Peep's bones.

The package in my mouth, I carry them to Karly. Why bother Auntie Heather when they're just as easy to take with us?

"George, I told you to *leave* it!" Karly doesn't sound very happy with me. For what might be the first time, she finds the spot where two shiny silver chain leashes are clipped together in our minds, the bond between us that was linked when Auntie Heather gave her to me. She shows me an image of me taking the bones back to where I found them. I snort. There are better uses for the link, but it's a good first try. Except, I am not going to do it. I picture her on the bike with the bandana pouch hanging from the handlebars.

"I don't think so." She drops her bike and goes after me. "Give!"

I shake my head and slobber flies all over the place. The bandana pouch wraps around my muzzle, making it harder for her to get if she's going to steal it. Karly wipes her face where some of my drool makes a direct hit. My Girlpup grabs my collar and it slips over my handsome head. She doesn't expect that, and falls back onto her rump. I walk onto her chest to make sure she's in one piece. Strings of drool drip onto her face. It's good to make her wake up.

"George! Off! Stop it!"

Oops, I guess she's awake. Hey, why's she laughing? An image shoots down our link. My wrinkly face, muzzle wrapped with a wet bandana, hanging over her face. Why is that funny?

Snort.

This is serious business.

"Fine. I give up. We'll take it to Auntie Heather." She pushes me off, dresses me in my collar, and hooks up her leash before she unwraps the bundle and takes it from me.

"I wonder what Auntie will think of your treasure. They can't really be human." Who's she trying to convince? My Girlpup ties the bundle to her handlebars and takes off for Auntie Heather's den. Karly is dragging me on the hot sidewalk forever. I like Auntie Heather's den, it's surrounded by big gardens. It's not the same as the woods, though, and it's far away.

Chapter Two

Huff, huff, huff. My mouth is dry as a new rawhide.

I need water.

Now.

Nownownow!

Karly forgets I am not built for speed—I am an energy-saving breed. She drags me by her leash while she rides her bike. Cough. Hack. Karly, I can't breathe! I think I should put the brakes on and sit with my legs out, but the road is pebbly. I don't like road rash and I like my tail, so I trundle behind her. At least it's cool. Spring's the best time. No time is good for running, though—unless there's a rabbit at the end of the run. There is no rabbit.

Sigh.

No rabbit.

It's a good thing that Auntie Heather's house is near the park where we were.

Pant, pant, pant.

I smell/taste tuna fudge. Auntie's strong herb/plant/cinnamon/Snickerdoodle smell/taste fills my mouth and nose.

She always knows when we're coming and makes me nummies. She's one smart Peep.

Drool.

Not as dry as I thought. My feet sound like thunder—badoom, badoom, badoom—on the sidewalk until I slide out of my collar, again. I break into a gallop and the sound turns to the racket of hail. There are nummies at the end. Karly tosses her bike on the car path and runs to the house after me.

"George! Slow down, you need to keep this on." My Girlpup holds out my collar, she's unsnapped her leash and it's hanging around her neck. I return to her and she buckles the collar back on. That's good; I feel naked without it.

We reach the big house. Auntie Heather opens the door and comes out onto the covered porch that wraps around her house. The screen door slams behind her with rattle. A metal bowl of water sloshes in her hands. It's not as yummy as in the toilet, but it smell/feels cold.

Excellent.

Put it down already. I stomple my feet to make my point clear. She frowns down at me, hair hanging over her eyes like an Old English Sheepdog, still holding my bowl, making a point to look at my paws.

Uh oh.

"When were your toenails cut last?" Her eyes track from my feet to Karly. I try to curl my toes under.

What's this thing with short toenails? My claws are tools. They dig, they scratch, they are important. They aren't meant to be short. Ugh. Auntie Heather is staring at me again. Wait a second, I'm magic. What if I think them into shortening a little? I put everything I can into my nails.

Nothing happens.

I think harder, my wrinkles folding on top of each other.

Still nothing.

I try one more time and peek down at them.

Nothing.

What good is magic if I have to accept the torture of nail trimming?

Auntie Heather finally places the water in front of me. I dunk my mouth and ears into the bowl and slurp as fast as I can.

"It's not torture and if we don't cut them they'll curl under and you won't be able to walk. Sometimes I wish magic worked for cleaning and grooming too—then I wouldn't have to dust and vacuum."

When I finish, I shake my ears dry. Ahhh, I needed that.

"Oh, yuck! George, you have a deadly aim," Karly says to me. Auntie Heather is still looking at my feet. I need a distraction. I nudge my Girlpup's hand.

Karly wipes her face and turns. "Oh yeah. Auntie Heather, look what we found!" She hands over the lumpy bandana pouch. "Are they human?"

What *we* found? Snort. Get real, young friend, I found them. You can't find anything under the ground even if you fall over it. I drink more of the sweet water and carry the last mouthful to Auntie Heather. I drop it on her feet to thank her for her thoughtfulness.

"You're welcome, George." She shakes her feet, one at a time.

The proper way to dry off.

Karly makes gagging noises. She doesn't even have a tight collar on to choke her.

"So, what did you bring me that you think could be human?" Auntie Heather opens the bandana pouch and looks at the bones inside. "Interesting. Oh, before I forget, did you bring my leopard's-bane and jewelweed?"

Auntie Heather waits while my Girlpup digs in her pack for the sack of plant bits and hands them over. "I didn't get a chance to get the jewelweed. We found the bones and thought we should show you right away. We can get the jewelweed tomorrow. I promise."

The smell/taste of tuna fudge makes my tummy rumble. There is a table where the porch stops. I want to mark the posts that hold up the roof, but they are on top of a short wall.

It's too high for me.

The smell/taste makes a strand of drool dangle from my mouth. When did I eat last? I don't remember, maybe never? I sidle up to Auntie Heather, sit, and give her pleading eyes. It's basset hound magic—resistance is futile. I drool at the thought of the tuna brownies. They smell wonderful, like sweetfishwarmsoftgooeygarlic.

My tail thumps in expectation. Auntie Heather is tall, even for a Ladypeep, and she squats next to me. Her dark hair has threads of a lighter color and she keeps it clipped back out of her eyes. It's poodle fur. She catches my image and laughs. I thump my tail even faster and roll over on my back. It's past time for belly rubbies.

Of course, Auntie Heather accepts my invitation.

I am totally irresistible.

"George, that's enough for now."

That means it's time for food, but she turns her attention to Karly.

I'm wrong? Fooooood...

"The bones look human. Put them over there on the table please, we'll know for sure with just a little work. Everything's all set up."

Karly's eyes are as round as cookies. "How'd you know what we'd be doing?"

Auntie Heather shrugs. "I saw it. I have tuna fudge for you, George. You already smelled them, didn't you, buddy?"

Is it that obvious? My drool is a waterfall.

"There are cookies and milk for you, sweetie. Did you call your mom to tell her you're going to be late?"

Karly looks at her aunt with stormy eyes.

"If you knew we were coming, why didn't you?" Karly's eyes instantly change from snit to sheepish. "I am sorry. I'll call her now. May I use your phone?"

Auntie Heather raises her brows. "Where's your cell?"

Karly bites her lip and speaks softly. "Um. I'm not sure. In the park, maybe?" "We didn't have time to find it." She points to me. "He went off and found these. Same reason we don't have the jewelweed. What good is his nose if he doesn't use it? Can noses have ADD?"

Auntie Heather sighs and gestures to the house. "You know where my phone is kept."

Karly takes off and the screen door clangs shut. I trot to the wood table, lock eyes on the tuna fudge, and whimper.

Drool.

Tuna fudge.

I feel more strands of saliva forming and shake them off. One of my ears flops over my head. Good, Auntie Heather can't put me off now. Peeps are always suckers for cute ears. "Aroo!" The fudge is mine.

"You did a good job with Karly today. Though, I wish you'd brought back the jewelweed. One of my friends needs it for her itchy skin." She sighs. "At least it's not an emergency."

Nodding my ear back, I whine. Tunatunatuna. I need less talk, more treat action. She gives in and tosses me a chunk. I catch it in the air—I am so coordinated. Woofing for another, she tosses me a tiny chunk. I gulp it down.

It's gone.

I gaze with my magic basset eyes for another. Auntie Heather holds up empty hands.

Oh, oh no!

"OwoooooOOoo." No! I'm sure I smell/taste more in the air.

Karly bounds back out of the house.

"'Kay. Mom says I can stay here until dinner, unless you want me to stay over. It's spring break, so I don't have to get up early." She gives our auntie 'basset eyes' almost as good I can. Karly likes Auntie Heather's food as much as I do, except for tuna fudge.

She has no taste.

"Oh, and she wondered if you had any fresh basil and lemongrass."

I know about grass. It's good when I need to throw up.

"Mom's making pesto tomorrow and hers don't grow as nice as yours."

Yum, pesto. What's pesto? Can I eat it?

"It's early yet. We'll see how long it takes and, if we need more time, I'll call Doreen and you can stay for dinner. Maybe we can give your mom and dad a night off and invite your brother. I haven't seen Joey for a long time. He's getting to be such a big boy."

Karly's jealousy of The Creep rolls over me like waves of bitter teabags. The bad part of being her familiar is feeling her emotions. She isn't usually so jealous of him. I know she's still angry she had to do his chores because he wasn't feeling well. "Are you ready?" They take seats at the table.

I sit at Auntie Heather's feet, but can't see anything. I jump up and put my paws on the table. A light colored crystal totters over and lands on my paw. "Yelp!"

"You don't belong at the table, George," says my Girlpup.

Snort that.

Auntie Heather grabs me by my collar and hauls me onto a chair. Now I can see the bones laid out in the center of a bunch of light and dark crystals. I can feel the energy that the witches can call from the rocks. It's tingly and smell/tastes like orange soda. I know because I sneak it from Karly's cup sometimes. I would like more.

"If we do this right, we can see how much living energy still remains in the bones. From that we can get a rough idea how old they are." Auntie Heather positions the crystals so they make crisscrosses through the remains.

This is ridiculous. I paw Auntie Heather's hand. My nose can tell how old the life scent is just as well as her crystals can, and I am faster! Karly says my nose has ADD. What's ADD? Packparents say Joey has ADD. My nose does *not*. It's perfect. "Woof!"

"Shhh, George. Yes, I know you can do this as well as we can. You could've tried without waiting for us. It doesn't matter, this is a fine learning

~ 16 ~

opportunity for Karly. She needs to learn how to do it herself, so she isn't dependent on you. All right?"

I sit in my chair and mope. Now that I know what they are, I can smell/taste more. The bones smell old, older than the bone I have buried in the backyard. They may even be from before breakfast time.

* * * *

Karly loves getting lessons from Auntie Heather. She found out she's a witch two years ago when she had her tenth birthday. The most magic moment in her life was when Auntie Heather gave me to Karly as a birthday familiar. I wish she could've started earlier, but witches need to bond to the Earthmom first. She was way too little back then.

The patio table is covered with a light tan cloth embroidered with various healing plants, phases of the moon, and stars. Scattered over the top are a lot of our auntie's favorite crystals. They range in size from a can of dog food to one of my claws. Karly is concentrating on the collection, trying to puzzle out what's necessary. A low soundfeel murmurs between the crystals. Gold threads sparkle between some stones, dead areas are between others, and some have weak connections. I catch Auntie Heather's eye and nod. My auntie is testing Karly. She moves a few—the thrum doesn't change. Some of the stones aren't needed and she knows it.

Auntie Heather bends into Karly, her face so close that even my Girlpup should smell the peppermints our auntie likes to eat. "Do you need help?" she asks.

Karly clenches her fists and bites her lip. She's searching the pattern. We both feel it isn't right, but she doesn't ask for help from Auntie Heather or me. She sucks in air and fills her lungs. She doesn't smell/taste anything, a waste if you ask me. As she slowly breathes out she lifts her hands over the collection of crystals. I see the colors through her eyes and she doesn't try to push me out. Now she needs what I see, too. There are areas with gaps where the energy isn't flowing right, sort of like sunshine on the dust that floats around my favorite chilling spot. The bad spots look like shadows.

Karly looks up and stops biting her lip. She collects stones that don't work and asks our auntie, "Is there any more red jasper? I don't need the rose quartz, amethyst, or the…citrine. That's it."

Auntie Heather takes away the crystals Karly doesn't want and hands her several shiny chunks of jasper. Still looking through Karly's eyes, I see the jasper is as deep red as raw meat. My stomach rumbles and both Peeps turn to look at me. I lower my head, hey, I haven't been fed in forever.

Karly is looking at the grid, her hands just above the setup. She bites her lip again and I hear her make a soft "hm" sound. She moves chunks of jasper and clear quartz. I feel the current of energy jolt through my Girlpup. I am proud of her, even if this is magic our auntie taught her. After all, I am getting to help. We feel bass vibrations, like from Karly's stereo speakers, run through us. She continues to move some of the stones until the pattern is in tune. Next, she carefully puts the bones in the center, each one the same distance apart.

"Do you remember what you're looking for?" Auntie Heather and I cock our heads. Karly snorts. She is feeling very confident. Well, I won't let her down, but let's see what she can do. She hasn't done this before. Neither have I, actually. I am the bone expert here, though.

Karly is very quiet as she puts her hands back over the top of her construction. I feeltaste the crystal energy bounce off the bone, and where there's lots of energy the bass vibrations are strong. I share the smell/taste of ice and heavy glass. She searches for any life-energy still in the bone. We feel there isn't much, only a small vibration and that's probably the spider weaving a web between a couple of the crystals. The bones are very old and very dead. Not fossil old, but still, the oldest things we've ever felt doing this kind of magic with our Auntie. Unlike the crystal grid, the faint spark of energy is the lighter tenor of Peeps. Mine is the same as my bay, a baritone. The color is exactly the shade of yellow as snow after I mark it. Karly groans at my thought.

"They're human and dead a long time. Now, how do I tell how old they are? Can I tell who they belonged to?" She's liking this and thinks it's like a cold case on one of the TV shows she watches. I sneeze, trying to get her attention. Hello, Girlpup, you can just ask me. I'll tell you more about them.

I have to get closer, so I stretch out and put my paws on the table. The chair is too far away and I thump to the floor. A tuna-smelling fart fills the room. Hey, I planned this. Yup, the floor is the place for a dog. I put my head on my paws

Auntie Heather waves her hands to make my perfume go away. She says to Karly, "We need to work with your ability to judge age better." She mutters, "Of course, to you everything is old, especially me."

She *is* old.

"It's harder to get the age of bones when they are this weathered unless the ghost is still around. Why don't you have George ask if he has any ghostly friends?" She drops her eyes to me lying on her feet. "Dogs often do. The energy feels less than a century to me. I'm thinking you have to do this the mundane way: research."

I raise my head and roll my eyes at her. She knows that ghosts don't like to hang around if they don't have to. They're only bits of Peeps. Besides, I would've told her already. Maybe I can talk to other ghosts.

Auntie Heather checks her watch. It didn't feel like we'd spent very much time, but it's already dark and I'm tired and hungry—we were out here for years.

"Help me put these things away and you can help me make dinner. I'll call your mom and then we can talk some more while we eat." She looks at her watch again. "Actually, I want to do some research. Would you mind terribly if I gave you a rain check and you can stay over another night? It's way too late to have Joey come over. Maybe next week."

I grin at that. I am not fond of The Creep. Karly puts up with him, but me, not so much. He likes to tease me by offering me food and eating it himself. He creeps on the floor and pokes me when I sleep. Creep is a good name for him. He also likes to tag along wherever we go.

Karly looks a little sad, but perks back up. "'Kay, maybe tomorrow? Oh, and remember, next week is Mom and Dad's anniversary. Bet they'd like a night away for a present."

Karly, why did you have to say that? I groan and roll my eyes, thunking my head down on Auntie Heather's feet. She gives me a look and pulls them from under me.

"I totally forgot. What a lovely idea! Their anniversary is what, Thursday? You two could sleep over. I'll call your mom and get everything settled after we're done cleaning up."

"What should I do about the bones?" Karly asks as she piles them in a box Auntie Heather hands her.

"Oh, just put them on the mantle in the living room," she says, carrying the larger pieces of crystal into the big stone den.

I like it.

If it didn't have huge windows, it'd be as good as a cave.

"No—" the door slams shut before Karly can finish her sentence. I get up, stretch, sit on Karly's foot, and thump my tail on the floor. She pushes me out of her mind.

I wrinkle my forehead and give her my patented 'Is it time to eat yet?' look.

"What?"

I just thump my tail harder. She slides her feet out and moves to the house.

"If you're worrying about dinner, I'm sure Auntie Heather has something for you to eat. Heck, she cooks for you. I'm surprised you don't come here every day."

"Arooo." I bolt for the door, moving in a rolling trot. I use my thick claws to scratch at the door. Auntie Heather needs to put a dog door in—the new scratches match the older marks I've made.

"George, really! Auntie Heather is going to have to replace the door if you trash it."

I look over my shoulder and pull my lips back into a full toothy grin. Joey thinks it's a snarl, but my Girlpup knows better.

She shakes her head. "I bet you think you're signing your work." She balances the box against the wall and pulls the door open. I squeeze by and nearly trip her. When I turn to check on my Girlpup, she narrows her eyes at me.

"Did you trip me in the park on purpose?

Uh-oh—busted. I present my rump and go into the house.

Karly follows me up the stairs. The living den is on one side. The important den is on the other. Karly goes into the living room. Sigh. The bones should be in the important room, where the food is made. She puts the bones away. Auntie Heather walks into the room, talking on the phone.

"Doreen, it's fine. I love having Karly here. She did great today. Oh, George and Karly found something interesting in the park. We're still doing some research, but it's very exciting. No, not sure about it yet. That's what makes it exciting. Yes, yes… I'll have her home right after dinner…Oh, I also have the herbs you wanted. I'll send them with her…Love you. Bye."

Auntie Heather turns to where my Girlpup is standing. "Bring in the rest of the stones and put them on top of the cabinet in the living room. I'll sort them later. Would you mind leftovers? I have stew or chili."

Yum! Both are nummy.

"Stew, please. What's George going to eat?"

At the same time they both say, "*Not Chili!*"

Oh, they think it's funny I am starving to death, do they? I go to the kitchen, walk to the fridge, and beat the seal with my paw. It pops open and I grab a bowl between my jaws. Auntie Heather is behind me and swipes it back. "Enough, George. You can have some of the stew, not all of it."

Chapter Three

Did I eat? I can't remember. My stomach growls. Where's my food? I smell stew, though there is none in my bowl. I stare up at Auntie Heather sitting at the kitchen table with Karly. She just laughs and ruffles my ears.

"Sorry, big guy, you've had enough. If you eat much more, you won't be able to get through the door. Karly, how much have you been feeding George? He's getting pudgy."

What? I am in perfect shape. I swing my butt around, aim, and let one rip.

Pffffffffft.

The scent breezes around me. It's delicate and earthy. I have graced them with one of my better ones.

"Auntie Heather! Did you give him the chili? Oh, for the sake of peanut butter and jelly. *No!*" Karly gets up and races to open the windows. I sit, not understanding the Peeps' reaction to my gift. I will never understand them. My Girlpup collects the plates from the table. *What is she doing*? Is she rinsing them in the sink?

No!

Mine!

Don't waste the goodness! "Nooaroooooo!"

"So where do I start researching? Missing persons pictures on old milk cartons? Find a ghost?" That's funny. I find ghosts. Karly doesn't see them.

Re-search?

Did we search before?

I sit on Auntie Heather's foot. I will stare at her until she remembers they forgot to feed me. I drool on her foot. Strands stick to her shoe. She pulls her foot out.

Fine.

I stretch out next to the table.

"I don't think milk carton pictures go back a century. There are a few finding spells we can perform if there are any possessions left from the person. Why don't you search the Internet? There might be some old newspapers that were put online."

"Were there newspapers back then?" Karly puts the last dish in the dish drainer. I clean plates better than she does. She didn't even share them.

"Yes, child, there were newspapers back then." Auntie Heather's snort makes some loose fur dance in the air. Papers are always around. Where else would puppies potty? A blob of something lands next to my head. I snap it up.

Hack.

Yuck.

A piece of clean napkin. Why not drop a used one? Those are tasty. I smell another piece. It *is* used. I suck it into my mouth.

"George, don't eat that," Karly says in a 'little kid trying to command me' voice. Hah, like that ever works. I clamp my teeth. "Give, George. You'll choke!"

I bite down, hard. She will give in. She will…

Auntie Heather drops a piece of tuna fudge in front of me. I drop the napkin and scarf down the treat. Bait and switch always works.

Back to re-search. I think ghosts can help. If Karly asks me nicely, I will do that for her. She seems to think it's better to yell at me to do what she wants.

Silly little Peep.

I hear chittering. Roquefort, Auntie Heather's raccoon familiar, struts in, like he owns the place.

Oh.

Yeah.

He does. His house. Where has he been? I sniff loudly. He smell/tastes of garbage. He smell/tastes of woods, and of fish and ponds. The smell/taste spreads over the roof of my mouth. Roque didn't tell me he was going on a field trip. I cry at his snub. "Arooo!"

"What's the matter with George? His howling is driving me nuts."

I feel Karly's glare on my back as I give a hard stare to Roquefort. I've known Roque for years and he should have taken me with him.

"Stop it, George! He's not doing anything to you." Auntie Heather always takes Roque's side.

Roque scrambles from the floor to a chair, to the table, and then up to my and Karly's auntie's shoulder. He settles in and chatters at me. I am not very good at speaking raccoon, but he tells me that he managed to soak something with pointy ears, a long tail, and sharp teeth. Sounds like him, but it's not, more like me. He soaked a dog? No? Whatever. While he's telling me the story he gestures with his little hands and laughs. I raise my brows and remind myself never to get on Roque's bad side.

"He thinks Roquefort got to do something he didn't get to. Now, George, you know that you were out in the woods today with Karly. You found the bones, after all." Auntie Heather looks out the window into the darkness. "Why don't I load your bike into the van and take you both home? You can plan how you're going to research who the bones belonged to. Maybe you'll be successful on the Internet."

Oh no, I hate it when Karly does computer stuff. She can't pet me if she's patting keys. Though there is a nice bed next to the desk. I like sleeping. I need a nap.

"That's a good idea. Any idea where to start? Sometimes key words are harder to figure out than the answer."

"Unsolved murders a hundred years ago since they feel about that old. Maybe that's too broad. You know, maybe you should see Mrs. Juniper at the library. Oak Prairie wasn't heavily populated back then. She might have some clues for you, like who lived on the property. I suppose I should've called the police. Oh well, I can call tomorrow. They'll need to talk to you, and your mom expects you home soon. It won't matter if the bones sit another day—they aren't in a rush, are they? Maybe the police will have some information on an old case. Stranger things have happened. Well, for now, go get the herbs for your mom and I'll take you two home before she worries. You have a lot you can do tomorrow. Oh, and George, if you go to the park, please show Karly the jewelweed."

I give them both a look and bay. My tail wags in a smiley face. That beats chilling next to the desk while Karly plays the keyboard. At least it doesn't sound as bad as when she plays on the piano.

Karly clips her leash to me and we head out to the garage. When she opens the car door, I jump into the front and take shotgun. Auntie Heather gets my Girlpup's bike and loads it into the back hatch. Karly tries to shoo me to the back. I sit and give her a predator's stare. She glares at me. I drool. She grabs my collar and tries to pull me over the seat back. How rude and unfair! I brace my front paws on the headrest and won't budge. Hah, I am too big for her to lift. She slams the passenger door and crawls into the back seat. I look over my shoulder and grin at her.

Chapter Four

We're in my den's kitchen. It's bright and my favorite room. I smell eggs and bacon, and drool and moan. There's only one thing that's wrong with this scene.

"Mooooom! Not fair, I want to go too," The Creep whines like a spoiled pug. He looks a little like one with his face all squished up like that. Karly called him Creep because he took a long time to walk. I call him that because he pulled my tail when he was just a little Boypup, and I try to stay far away from him. He still takes my food and hides it so he can 'train me to use my nose'.

As if I need such a thing.

I have mad nose skills that are far beyond his feeble attempts to trick me. With luck Mom will say no to his tagging along. My life is perfect except for The Creep.

"Karly, is there any reason he can't? It's rather exciting, you finding those bones like that."

I bark in my finest song-voice, reminding her it was my mighty nose that discovered the treasure. My Girlpup can't find her clothes in the morning.

"Yes, George, I see you."

I wag my tail. My part in this should be rewarded. "Boof."

"Heather noticed you're gaining a bit of pudge around the middle. Sorry big guy, it's time to back off on the treats. Long dogs with short legs don't need to be fat—it's bad for your back. We don't want you hurt, do we?"

Hurt? I'll show her hurt. I roll over on the bright yellow tile, submitting to the dark-haired Packmom who controls my supper dish. I try to make my tummy rumble. It produces a small gurgle. I think no one hears it except me. Stupid stomach, it doesn't get the game. She bends over and pats my beautiful white belly, but that doesn't fill it. I flop back over when Packmom straightens up.

Karly isn't happy. Her eyes are slits as she looks at our common pest. "Mom, it's going to be hard enough to talk to the police. Joey will talk their ears off." Her arms are crossed over her chest, her chin up. Be strong Girlpup, we don't need The Creep with us.

Mom puts an arm around her Boypup. "Joey, do you promise to not bother your sister? You can't interfere with the police investigation, or I'll have to come get you. Do you understand?"

Joey nods. "I'll be good, promise Mom." I know he lies. Peeps are quite good at that. I walk to him and drool on his shoe. It strings down and hits his foot. For some reason he grimaces and gets paper towels and wipes his shoe. I should lift my leg on him, but I know better. It means the crate if I am that naughty. I have better things to do. I will ignore him. I stick my nose in the air and turn away from him.

"Fine, he can come. He better stay away from me though." Karly gives in.

I don't need mind reading skills to hear the threat behind the words. What is 'or else'?

* * * *

"Arooo!" I bay in my magnificent full voice. There's a Peep with a shiny badge here in Auntie Heather's living room. They usually live in cars that try to bay as beautifully as me—silly Peeps—there is nothing with a voice as beautiful as mine. I smell sweet gun oil, bitter powder, and sharp metal. There is a gun on his belt. I love the scent of guns. They kill rabbits for me. Are there rabbits?

No.

This is the house. There aren't rabbits in the house. My forehead wrinkles as I sigh.

"Shut up, George, if I have to be good, so do you," Joey says. He is a snot. I woofle at him and scare him off. He walks away.

I am a good boy and don't jump on the Badge Dude. I want to. The Badge Dude is sitting on my big brown bed they call a couch next to Auntie Heather.

I paw him. I don't mind sharing, but he's taking all my space. He doesn't shift over even a little. Karly is sitting on a low table. Joey is in the kitchen getting treats. He won't let me in the kitchen with him.

I grumble under my lips.

"So your niece, let's see, Karly is it?" The Badge Dude looks at my Girlpup. She nods. That means she agrees. I understand Peep language better than Peeps understand dog. The Badge Dude continued, "So Karly found this pile of human bones? Why didn't you call earlier?"

What? I found the bones! Why am I always forgotten?

Peeps are slow.

I woof to remind the Peeps I am here. Although, thinking about it, I do learn a lot listening and watching them.

"George dug them up. I just figured they were animal bones. This morning Aunt Heather thought it was better if we called and made sure. We didn't want to bother you if they were just deer bones." Karly sort of stuttered through her words.

Auntie Heather rescues Karly from repeating that she was sure they were animal bones. "May I get you something? I have coffee, water, or pop. And I just finished baking a batch of Snickerdoodles. They're still warm." She uses the cajoling voice; the same one that she uses when she wants me to do something I don't want to do.

Hey.

Did she share any with me?

No.

I walk over to her and put a paw on her knee. I can smell the mug of hot cocoa Karly carries to a light-colored chair—along with Snickerdoodles.

No Snickerdoodles for the loyal dog.

My Girlpup ignores me. I sit on her foot. Feed me, and your foot will be released. I will her to drop the cookie with my eyes. She resists my awesome power. Mousefleas. It's the bond between familiar and witch—we can't influence each other.

"I'm good that you called, except you should've called immediately. I'll admit, though, finding what might be human bones isn't exactly typical. I might think they belonged to an animal as well." The Badge Dude smiles at Karly. Sure, when I show my teeth and grin, everyone runs away. That's doggy discrimination. Any smart dog knows the difference between a snarl and smile. Few humans seem to. The Badge Dude turns his head, sneezes, and pulls air through his nose.

Humph.

Stupid way to smell/taste.

"Well, if you find more bones, make sure you call right away. I need to have you take me out there now. We're fortunate that it didn't rain last night, the forecast called for heavy thunderstorms."

I cast a look at The Badge Dude. He's like a big, stupid, black Labrador. Even Labs use their noses. If he'd used it, he would have smelled that the sweetwatermelonscentcool of rain was missing in last night's air. I shake out my ears.

Peeps.

They have noses, yet they do not smell. They have skin, yet they do not feel. I think Roque told me that. Maybe his nose is stuffy. Maybe he has allergies. He sneezes again and looks for something. Auntie Heather hands him a nummy tissue box. The Badge Dude takes one, honks into it, and holds it. I cruise over and nudge his hand. This is tasty stuff. Auntie Heather offers a wastepaper basket and he tosses it in. Rats.

Well, even if he can't smell, the bones are old! Not like they'll find anything useful. I didn't, and I have superior senses. "Arooo!" I inform them. I can take you. Don't expect much from Karly. Maybe she'll get lucky and step on a rabbit hole. I love bunnies!

"I think George can help you. Karly, when you, Joey, and George are out there, can you look for jewelweed? I really need it for my salve."

The Creep runs into the living room like a frightened mouse. I want to pounce on him. I am too dignified for such things and hold back.

"Joey, no running in the house," Aunt Heather scolds. I woof at him to make sure he understands.

I hear the rub of pant legs as The Badge Dude moves to the window that shows the garden. "George is a beautiful basset hound. I had one as a kid, Stanley. Stubborn, but smart." The Badge Dude's voice is deep. Not bad, he would bay well—maybe, just maybe, I could teach him.

He walks to where I'm sprawled next the couch, watching with my head still on Karly's foot. The Badge Dude bends and pats the top of my head. I hate that. My brow wrinkles and I press my head into his hand. Massage, it's what we dogs like. He wouldn't like me to pat his head. It causes headaches and it's not like I can ask for the stuff the Peeps use to cure theirs.

At least until Karly keeps our link open.

He rumples my ears. Not bad. His basset should have trained him better. Maybe he forgot.

"Can you get him to take us to where you found the bones?" Like he has to ask? "I remember that Stanley wasn't the best at focusing and I don't know if that's the norm for bassets." What is wrong with this dude? I shake him off.

"Grawf." I get up and pull Karly's leash off the door. When I drop it at the Badge Dudes feet, he picks it up and smiles.

"Well, that's telling me off." The Badge Dude massages my ears. My tail sways back and forth with appreciation. My body melts into his hand. "All right, let's meet in the parking lot." The Peep gets up and leaves.

"Let's take the car, I don't want to keep him waiting," Auntie Heather says. I approve with a wide grin. If Karly drags me I won't smell/taste as well as I will need to. My throat hurts and I can't smell/taste for a while. Coughing doesn't improve my abilities as a tracker. Karly hooks the leash to me so she won't get lost. I lead her to the garage and she opens the door for me. This is proof she can learn from me. I pull her to the car. Hurryhurryhurry, I bark. He will get there before us! Joey opens the front passenger door and slides in. No way! Mine! I jump on his lap, my claws digging into his bare legs.

"Karly, your dog is scratching me! Make him stop. Pee-yew! What're you feeding him? He smells!"

"Get out of his seat, then. He likes to look through the front window. Besides, it keeps him from getting sick and barfing."

Hey, Girlpup, I haven't been car sick in a couple of years. The Creep slides out from under me. Karly did good, she can be smart about reading Peeps.

Auntie Heather is behind us, locking up. It's an acknowledgement that she doesn't need to protect her things while I am around. She is a smart witch and I stop barking.

It has absolutely nothing to do with Karly telling me to shut up.

The car's tires always smell burned. When I went under a car to chase a mouse as a pup, the Peeps made me take a bath to get rid of the greasy black gunk. I don't like baths, so I avoid going under cars. I like going for rides with my head out the windows. My ears gather the tastesmell from the wind and I can feel the pressure of the weather on my nose.

It's *wonderful*.

"Aroo." My Peeps look at me. I turn my head. Let's go already!

* * * *

It takes forever to get to the park. I can't sleep because The Creep keeps touching Karly. Why does he get to come? He's a big pain in my rump. The car ride is horrible. I fart over the seat back, and then look at The Creep like he did it. At least the windows are open and I can hang my head out and enjoy the wealth of smell/tastes. Auntie Heather is a patient Peep, or she's good at ignoring us. I bet she's ignoring us.

"What does the officer think we'll find? I told them we found everything out there." Karly grumps out. "Adults don't listen to kids."

"I'm listening. I'm also thinking. This is just so fascinating. Witches usually heal people, not find out what killed them. I hope we can solve this. Joey, in the five minutes it's taken to get to the park from your house, you've poked your sister forty-three times. That is quite enough." Auntie Heather is cheerful no matter what the Pups are doing. I am hoping she's cheerful because she's planning on taking Joey home.

"Do you think maybe I'll find some bones? Huh? I want to find some bones!" Joey's voice is high and goes right through my eardrums. "Arrrrrrooooooooooooo." Auntie Heather better do something with him or I won't be able to hunt because I'll have a headache.

"Joey, indoor voice please. If anyone is going to find bones, it's the one with the nose," Auntie Heather tells The Creep. "Your job is to watch and learn from the police. Perhaps we can compare the differences between what you see on TV and real life. You will *not* interrupt their work, unless you want to go home. Got it?"

Joey scowls at her and nods his head. He runs his fingers over his lips and tosses the "key".

At Karly.

Right.

That will make things better.

If I could just bite him. Just a nip…

Auntie Heather rolls her eyes and pulls into the parking lot. We pull in behind a light blue and white police car with squiggles painted in navy on the side.

Before he even opens the door, Joey asks non-stop questions. "How come the lights are flashing? Where's the yellow tape? How come there's only one car?" He doesn't even take a breath until Auntie Heather interrupts.

Blue and yellow are good colors. They smellfeel tingly like the wind in my ears. They aren't loud like the colors that shout at Peeps. It's not fun to look through my Girlpup's eyes.

"Karly, I'm going to let you and George out. I'll be back after I drop Joey off at your house." Joey howls. I bark with glee, but our auntie pins me with her Alpha stare. I stop and hang my head so my ears cover my eyes. I don't want her to know I am happy about Joey. She taps my nose. As if I can hide anything from her.

The door locks unlatch and I hear seat belts snap open. I jump out and shake out my coat and aiming drool at The Creep. Oops. Some hits the police car. I take a huge breath. I don't smell The Bad Thing. Aunt Heather mouths she'll be right back, and drives away.

Good.

No more Joey.

Now, where's the Badge Dude?

I sniff the air, turning my head to look up at Karly with soft brown eyes. Heh, I take off before she can put her leash on and weigh me down. I bark and head to the woods. Karly grumbles the same words at me that she used for Joey in the car.

Chapter Five

The Girlpup still hasn't learned how important time is. She finally figures out I am not waiting and follows me. I can smell the Badge Dude is near the bone place. Well, and I see the ground is more stompled in their direction. Karly keeps calling my name. No time to waste, if they think there are more bones then I will find them. I smell rabbit. I shake my head, no time for rabbit now. I drop my head low to the ground, my ears fall forward and my lovely neck wrinkles roll down to form a scent-scoop. Maybe they are right and there are more bones here. Maybe they're good-tasting bones and not Peep bones.

I inhale. There is something gassulfurdrysnakecatstink not-right in the air. Did I smell this before? I sniff more deeply.

The scent is gone.

Hehhehhehhehh. I pant and circle around the spot.

Nothing.

Where is it? What the heck is it?

"Arrooo," I bay in frustration. Did the Wrong-thing take my bones?

Karly calls me. Her heavy feet crunch and crush the plants, the smell/taste of bitter things fills my nose. Good, she's following; I don't need to worry she's lost my stealthy path. Maybe she can finally read a trail. More likely she's lucky. I shake out my ears to get rid of the earlier scents as I come closer to the Badge Dude. The strange gassulfurdrysnakecatstink scent is here. It's so thick I can't understand why I missed it yesterday. It isn't anything I've smell/tasted before. If I smell/tasted it yesterday I wouldn't have grabbed the bones. I want to cover my nose. Instead, I gather more of the scent in my folds and savor it, chewing it over like a beef bone.

Nothing.

It doesn't spark any memories for me. I turn around, scuffing my paws a little, hoping to turn up more scent clues. Nothing other than that bad smell fills my nose and covers my tongue. I want water. I want…Karly! Karly is near the thing. The fur on the back of my neck prickles, making me look bigger. I run to her, baying, barking, yelping. It's theretherethere. Karly! I rush to her.

She trips over my back.

"Why do you always have to trip me, you blockheaded freak? Look where you're going and don't run into me," she shouts. My ears and tail droop and my tail stops wagging. Why yell at me? I am her protector. Her auntie tells me every time we see her—it's my duty. I must protect her from the Bad Thing I don't recognize.

"Sniff."

Still nothing.

All I smell/taste are Karly's anger and the Badge Dude. Is it scared away? I hope so. Karly doesn't understand there is something bad out here.

I put my nose back to the ground and continue to inhale. There's a patch of sweet grass. I bite off a mouthful, enjoying the tearing as I rip and chew. More scents come from the ground.

A squirrel.

My ears rise, my nose quivers.

No, I'm *not* here for squirrels. Or the bouquet of chipmunks, bunnies, cats, deer that flows over my nose and tongue.

Drool.

Musky, bloody from a kill, hawk leftovers.

No, no, no. I shake my head before I lower it again. My loose skin and ears fall forward catching up the lovely scent. I ignore the wonderfulness and search for something not normal.

The gassulfurdrysnakecatstink smell/taste is weak. I follow the trail until it's stronger and new. There are other scents that shouldn't be here—drybitterdust of broken plates and glass. The sharphardtang of cold, old metal. More bones, not tasty. Not new. Oh no, more Peeps' bones. I feel bad. These were Peeps that could feed and pet me and now they are gone.

I trot to Karly, butt her leg with my muzzle and boofle. I have news. She shakes me off.

Figures.

Auntie Heather is back without The Creep. I walk over to her. Concentrating hard at her, we connect in a way that Karly needs to learn.

I try to teach her, though she's not always a good student.

"Yes, George, you're a very good teacher and familiar. It's hard; she's becoming a teenager you know," Auntie Heather croons quietly to me as she bends down to ruffle my ears. I curve my head into her hand. No, I don't know about this teenager thing. Is it something to do with Karly's new smells? "Now, what did you find?" Aunt Heather asks.

As best as I can, I let her smell/taste what I found. She looks at me oddly. "That is different; I wonder what you found. Excellent boy. Good job. Lead me to the trail." She pats her leg, as if I need encouragement. This is important, my Pack must be kept safe. Grrr. I will get The Bad Thing and kill it, or make it go away forever. Grrr. Now I am angry it dares come on my territory. I lift my leg on the closest weed and pee on it. I slowly walk with Auntie Heather, leading her and peeing on trees until my tank is almost empty.

Mine.

'This whole place is mine,' I say by pee-mail. Stay away. I bay a warning just in case it can hear me.

I almost step into a hole. It smells rotten and I hack before my mouth fills with the scent. I look more closely at it. The hole isn't a hole—it's a big footprint, as big as two of my own paws, and I am no slouch in the foot department. The smell/taste puddles in the top of the print and settles in the long deep grooves at the top.

Claw marks.

I look for more of the prints.

None.

Where are the other four? Is it a pogoing Bad Thing?

There are trees all around and I want to lift my leg again.

Only a trickle. Mousefleas, well, it's enough, anyway. I drop my leg and notice scratch marks shredding the bark of the tree. It's the kind that sometimes drops lots of round seeds on my head. It climbs. That's why I sometimes get the scent, and sometimes it's faint or gone. This is one time that Karly's looking up is useful. I jump up and lean against the tree. "Aroooo!" Come on Karly, Auntie Heather, comecomecome, see what I've found!

Auntie Heather is first and sees the scratches, bark hanging in strips. She raises her hand and pets the bark and grooves.

"Poor tree. It looks almost like buck rub, but they do that in fall. What on Earth?" she says. Her face is sad. I fall back to my paws and press my gorgeous self on her legs. That always makes her happy. Auntie Heather is very soft and hurt living things make her upset. I can fix her.

Most of the time.

Like now.

She smiles down at me and sees The Bad Thing's print. Oh. Yeah. Almost forgot. I snuffle at it, letting her know I see it, too.

The loud crashing sound tells me Karly is coming even though she is downwind. We'll need to work on stealth. She'll never catch a bird at this rate.

When Karly gets closer I "aroo" to get her attention—she needs to hurry up and see this. It's importimportimportant! I jump around to attract her attention, making as much a racket on the leaves and sticks as she does. It's kind of embarrassing, actually. Karly sees me and frowns.

Or, not at me.

She's brushing off sticky spider webs. It'd be better if she'd save them. They are good for bandages. Auntie Heather gives me a smile as she strokes a tree with heart-shaped leaves. She agrees. The tree's bark is ruined. It won't heal without some help.

The area stinks like The Big Bad Thing. What is it? I don't know of any animals that scratch like that in the spring. No lightning storms here in forever.

This is a clue.

To what?

"What made those?" Karly asks. I push the gassulfurdrysnakecatstink smell/taste into her mind and chortle. Even when it goes straight to her brain she can't interpret what she smells. She only gets the smell/taste of her brother's room, and snakes. "Oh, yuck. George, you didn't have to share."

I shake my head. She could use her nose, as poor as it is. Auntie Heather needs to remind my Girlpup that I am her teacher. I poke my nose into the print. Karly comes closer and investigates.

"Wow. That is the biggest print I've ever seen. It's so round, like an elephant's foot with claws." She holds her hand over it like she's comparing the sizes. "Maybe it isn't a print. Maybe it's something else." She doesn't sound convinced.

I snoofle the ground for more.

Nothing. I hate only getting nothings from the monster.

What walks on only one foot?

"That's can't be…that's not a ginormous paw print, is it?" she asks my auntie. "What made it?"

That, Girlpup, is a good question. Now, leave me alone so I can investigate. I don't need special tools, either.

Is that the trail? There are so many leaves, when was there a windstorm? I am excited, and stop in front of a pile of fresh green leaves mixed with old brown leaf skeletons. I flex my paws and scrape at the ground, my thick claws and wide feet tearing it up, flinging everything under my butt. I hear Karly shout out, and tuck my head between my front paws to look behind me.

Whoops.

Karly is directly behind me. Dirt and leaves cover her head.

"George, I mean it; I'm going to hang you by your ears from the clothesline. You're doing that on purpose."

I decide her comment is beneath my notice and dig faster. I stop to investigate each piece as some broken wedges of dirty plates fly out of the hole, and a dull silver knife. Good thing it's dull. I nose the thing and dig even faster. Maybe there is food on another piece.

"Oh my. I think I'll go get the police officer. He should see this," Aunt Heather says as she pats the tree one more time and heads back to where the bones are. So, why didn't the Badge Dude follow us? I know where the important stuff is.

I stop digging when only dirt comes up and turn to investigate my pile.

Hmmm.

There's a fork, something that looks like a thick curved straw with a little hole, some buttons, a metal mug, and more bits of plate.

No food on it.

Mousefleas.

Karly grabs a stick and stirs my treasures with it. Hey! Stop it, they're important. I stand in front of them. She pushes me away. "George, it's all useless junk." She picks up one of the plate pieces I cleaned. "I can't believe you licked that, it's nasty.

"What is so important that you dragged us over here to look at this. A bunch of scratches, a footprint, and a junkyard. Not a single bone. George, you're a blockheaded freak."

That's her special pet name for me. The treasures are mixed with dirt so I nudge them out into a separate pile. Karly says "squirrel" in her mind and I swish my tail. It forms a lovely crescent down my back.

"George, unless it's an emergency I don't want you reading my mind. There isn't a squirrel except for you."

Oh sure.

Go ahead and tease me.

There's a ruffle of leaves as Peeps walk through them. They aren't quiet, but compared to Karly they sound like a breeze in the trees. I am still in her head and she rolls her eyes at me. "'Kay, yeah, I'll try to be more quiet. It would be nice to see animals instead of just prints."

I shudder. She shouldn't meet The Bad Thing.

Not ever.

The adults gather around my treasures.

"So what do we have here? Any more bones?" The Badge Dude points to my pile. He crinkles his forehead and grabs Karly's stick to move some things out of the pile. There are seven round things, some are black and some are brown. They smell like metal. Only puppies eat metal.

"Interesting. Looks like old American coins. Where would they come from? George, are there more?"

Karly is shaking her head and isn't happy. Maybe she wanted the Badge Dude to ask her? How would she know? I snuffle, scrape the ground, snuffle more, and sit down.

More nothing. "Aroooo!" I bay in frustration.

"These things may not have anything to do with the bones, but I trust the dog. He's the one with the nose." The Badge Dude bends down and strokes my back. It's only friendly to put my paws on the cop's shoulders and lick him on the face.

"George, *off*!" My Girlpup thinks she can command me? I turn my head away and ignore her. I'm thinking she's glaring at my neck.

"It's fine." The Badge Dude pushes my front paws off his shoulders and places them on the ground. "You shouldn't jump up, though, that can't be good for your back." That's nice he's concerned for me. He straightens up and looks around. He sees the hurt tree and walks over, cocking his head to each side like a big bird. He walks around the tree, less than two of me away, before reaching out to touch the shreds of bark.

"These look fresh. Any idea what caused the gouges?" he asks. I am not sure if he's asking my auntie, Karly, or me.

Aunt Heather avoids the paw print as she moves to the tree. "I honestly don't know. It's too early in the year for buck rub, and unless you've had some reports of big cats or bears, there isn't anything else that would do that. Certainly nothing that has a print like this." She points to the print. The Badge Dude bends over it and gives a low whistle.

"I've never seen anything like this and I hunt up north every fall." He lifts his dark blue cap with one hand and scratches his head with the other. "I'm going to call in some people. In the meantime, we'll be closing off the area for a while. Thanks for coming out."

"Will you tell us what you find?" Our auntie asks. "We are organizing a few more demonstrations to keep the park, but we don't want to get in the way of an investigation. In a way, I guess, this might help keep the bulldozers out of the woods for a while."

That's our auntie. She can make lemonade out of…well, nothing. She has mad skills that way. Take old Peep bones, some junk, stir well, and she's made soup. It's a type of magic Karly wants to learn badly. Well, she has some of the badly part down pat. I have no doubts she'll improve with me as her familiar.

"When I find something, I'll let you know what I can." Badge Dude is grinning at her. What is that all about? I look at Auntie Heather. There's nothing to grin at here—time to move along.

Aunt Heather motions that we can go. "Let's go back to the house. It's a lovely day to work on healing spells and green magics."

Karly's smile is bright enough to light up the hole I dug. She is nearly jumping up and down. "What kind of healing magic?"

"You'll see when we get to my house. This is a special kind of healing that I'm sure you're ready for."

I think we should spend some time doing park magic. I know what the big trucks in the parking lot are going to do. I don't like it. Witches have protected it forever, keeping the lands and plants healthy. Does Aunt Heather really think the bones and junk could help? I don't see how. I pant my way to the car. Shotgun!

"Hurry up slow-poke. George is already waiting next to the car. What are you daydreaming about?" I hear with my super hearing. They could move a little faster. I think about taking a nap.

Karly is still walking slow, looking at the trucks. "I was just wondering how we're going to save the park. Do you think it's too late?" She points to the things that destroy the land, and garbage containers in the parking lot.

Aunt Heather shakes her head as she unlocks the door to the car. "It's never too late. Our family has preserved these woods for generations, keeping out what doesn't belong, saving what does. It's not going to be so easy for anyone to damage it and I suspect this is just what we need."

Karly's face scrunches in confusion. "How? It's just junk. The police will figure out who the bones belong to and that will be it. How can that save our park?"

I sneeze and leap into the shotgun seat. You snooze you lose. I paw the window to remind Auntie Heather it needs opening.

My eyes go round when I hear Karly practically growl, "Oh no you don't. I sit in front—you sit in back. Auntie Heather, if I have to wear a seatbelt, why doesn't he?"

Aunt Heather points to the back. I drop my head and crawl between the seats. "That's not a bad idea. I've seen them at the Pet Food Emporium, I'll pick one up the next time I need food for Roquefort."

I give a good shake and spray drool everywhere once I am in the back. That's better. Next, I try to turn three times before I lie down. The seat's too narrow. I thump down on the seat with a sigh. The seat groans and Auntie Heather turns around to look at me.

"Maybe I'll get a seat cover too. For a short-coated dog he sheds a lot. His fur's weaving into the fabric. Some of my friends are allergic to dogs, and sometimes I need to drive them to spots of power to heal them. This park has the best one in the area—the water carries a lot of energy. Remember, we saved the old covered bridge. It's such a lovely site and the perfect place to do healing ceremonies. So much healthy energy."

There is plenty of energy everywhere. The river is a magical place, so are the hills. I never did understand why my witches seem to think running water is all that. It's okay. The water is stained brownish except where it rushes over large, rounded boulders that look like Swiss cheese.

And now the destruction Peeps want to build houses along the river.

"What are you feeding George now?" My auntie asks. I am trying to snooze and a few poots escape me. She rolls down the windows.

"I don't know. Mom gets it at the grocery store. He likes it. Maybe too much, I don't think he chews when he eats."

"Remind me to talk to your mother about getting him on a better diet. I can pick up a premium food for him at the Emporium while I'm there. A healthy familiar is a stronger familiar."

Food is good.

Chapter Six

The car bumps up the driveway and wakes me. I didn't get to stick my head out the window. Mousefleas. I put my paws on the door and woof so they let me out. They might forget me.

"No one could forget you. Let me get out first." Auntie Heather laughs as she unbuckles herself from the seat. They don't really have seatbelts for dogs, do they? I don't want to wear one. It's beneath my dignity. Besides, how could I lean out the window and inhale the bouquet of sweet smell/tastes in the wind? These are the hot colors of life. No way anyone is making me wear a seatbelt. I sit back and my tail thuds against the back of the seat.

Karly is out before me. Openopenopen the door, I bark at her. She ignores me. When will she understand we're a team? Auntie Heather clacks the door open and I hop out. A quick shake to get my fur into place and I am ready to rock and roll.

And eat.

I snuffle, but I don't smell anything. Oh yeah, Auntie Heather is with us. I give her my puppy eyes and look to the door. I think food and worm the thought into her head. Karly needs to open her mind to me like this.

"I have some carrots. You really have a one-track mind sometimes. Karly, there are some herbs in a basket on the dining room table. Why don't we go into the gazebo and work out there? It's too pretty a day to waste it inside. Besides, the magic is stronger out here near the soil."

Karly goes into the house. I follow Aunt Heather out to the garden. She yanks up some orange crunchy bones. I try to take them, but she softly hits me on the nose with them. "You might not mind eating dirty carrots, however I'm not too fond of you kissing my mouth when you thank me."

This is confusing. She spends most of her time taking care of the Earthmom and she doesn't like it in her mouth? I wait for her to rinse them off under the hose and paw her leg because she's not fast enough. I woofle under my breath. Come on already, you're slower than worms and they are only good for rolling on.

It takes her forever to rinse them under the hose before she gives them to me. I take them without nipping her fingers and go lay under the big tree to chew. Sweetcrunchiness, they are gone too quickly. Auntie Heather and Karly sit in the gazebo surrounded by plants. Flowers are filled with bees, following stripes on the petals into the stickysweet mouths of the flowers. The bees are lucky the flowers don't trap them. I respect bees, they like to bite noses and they don't use teeth. The flying bugs use stingers that hurt like the shots at the vet. I shake a little. Auntie Heather told me vets are important healers and while she can do a lot, the vet can help her keep me healthy.

I guess.

That doesn't mean I have to like shots.

"George! Are you deaf or what? Get your butt over here, Aunt Heather says I need you," my partner in crime sweetly bellows.

I look around first for missing carrot bits.

Nope.

My name is rudely spoken again by the Girlpup. Hold your horses—speed isn't everything. Nevertheless, I shift gears and trot to the gazebo.

Hey, it's not a walk.

My claws tap as I climb the wooden steps and go into the shelter. I spy a bowl of water and gulp some down. When I lift my head, I notice tiny bits of floating carrots. I try to get them, but inhale water instead. Karly is sitting near so I wipe my face on her convenient jeans and snort water out of my nose.

"George!"

What? I don't see a towel anywhere. What am I supposed to do? I look at her with my cutest expression. She glares and pushes me away.

"So why do I need..." Karly jabs her finger in my direction, "It?"

It?

It? I dip my head and look between my legs at my private bits. All there. Whew. Never call a dog an "it"; it's cruel. I snort in her general direction and move to where Auntie Heather is sitting at the heavy, black metal table. I slump into a sit and slowly ooze into a down. Her foot makes a great pillow.

"Teamwork. You will learn to pool George's and your energy together to perform the more difficult healing for both animals and the land. If you have the gift, you might even be able to see the future or the past with your familiar's help. If it turns out you're a seer, I'll get Phoebe to help with those lessons."

My Girlpup's eyes get very round and she dips her head down to me, and then up to Auntie Heather. "Do you think I might have that gift?" she squeals. Make my head ring, why don't you, Karly?

"I don't know what you might manifest. Right now your future is a vast plain waiting to be planted. Far-seeing is a hard gift, though. You can't take back what you've seen, no matter how horrible it is or was. The path might be re-shaped, but the scene will still remain as a memory. From what I hear, it's not like watching television. Even if it doesn't come to pass, it still feels like you were there, a part of it. Truly, a gift with a sharp double-edged blade."

It doesn't seem like it would be a bad thing to see the future.

Food in the future.

Food in the past.

Unless...*No!* I wouldn't like to see an empty supper dish. I hope Karly and I never get that, um, puppy present. I am embarrassed to find myself shaking and roll over, exposing my tummy. Karly surprises me by kneeling down and rubbing it. I think she isn't any happier than I am with the idea. I settle and snuggle against her bent leg. She sits cross-legged and I drape myself over her lap. She smell/tastes wonderful—grape Koolaid, and sweetsweat, not quite tangy like adults, warm. She's mine, part of my Pack. She lets me stay and I deflate with a sigh.

She changes the subject. "What are we going to do?"

"I thought a little healing magic to start with. Rupert, here, fell out of the big hickory and hurt his leg this morning. He isn't very happy in the splint. Perhaps you can help get him out of it." While I was half-snoozing on Karly, Auntie Heather must've gotten up. There's a box on her lap and I smell fleas and dead trees...*Squirrelsquirrelsquirrel!* Why is there a squirrel on Auntie's lap? It's dangerous. It will eat her! I jump up and lunge for Auntie's lap.

"Down, George, he's only a baby. Beneath you. He'll be good to practice your paws, um, I mean, hands-on healing," Auntie Heather says while using one hand to support the box and the other to push me away. I put my butt down and glare at her. I am going to heal a future killer?

So wrong.

I turn my head away and think about leaving.

My Girlpup squeals in my ear. I hold back the bay of frustration. Karly is too excited about the rat with a fuzzy tail and won't listen to reason. Instead, she reaches for the evil ball of fur and carefully removes it from the box. I decide to go home and am turning-tail when Auntie Heather stops me.

"George, you are a brilliant familiar, and have so much to share with Karly, don't you? But first you have to teach Karly how to heal and Rupert here literally fell into my lap. Can't you accept the challenge of healing him in order to teach your student?"

My head hangs between my front legs, embarrassed. Karly needs my help and wisdom, not my prejudice, even if it is well-founded. I look at the fluffy-tailed rat, and it blinks its beady little eyes at me, happy in my Girlpup's hand. It's taunting me! I growl. Auntie Heather gives me a sharp glance and I look away from the demon-spawn.

Auntie Heather continues, "I know that George and you don't always see eye-to-eye, but dogs make great familiars for witches. Dogs are natural healers. Just petting them makes high blood pressure drop. Roquefort has many wonderful qualities, however he also has some drawbacks. For example, most hospital staff don't want a 'wild animal' in the patient's room. Besides, he's shy around crowds."

It's good that Auntie Heather points out my special super-powers. Peeps help us hunt and herd. We get the food—they prepare it and serve us. It's part of our job to keep Peeps calm and safe, slowing their heartbeats to match our breathing patterns as they pet and cuddle us. That's easy stuff. Any dog can do that. I am more than a dog, though. I'll show my Girlpup. We'll make that squirrel so healthy I'll be able to chase it in no time.

I rub my muzzle against Auntie Heather's leg and creep over to Karly and the furry-tailed rat. It blinks at me and I feel its pain in my own leg. My mom shared the great truths with me, except I must not have paid attention during this part. I sure don't remember it was going to hurt. I whimper and lick my front leg. There is a dirty brownish glow around the owie and I concentrate on it. My colors are shiny yellow and sunny-day blue.

Slipping into Karly's mind, I show her what I'm seeing. She looks at my leg, confused. The furry-tailed enemy squirms and she drops her gaze to it. Its leg is surrounded with a darker version of the glow and there is a frayed, twisted cord leading from the squirrel to me. I want to bite it, but that would just leave me and squirrel both hurting. I woof. Does she see what she needs to do, or should I show her?

Since Karly looks like she's doing a math problem, I decide to show her. My tongue lolls out of my mouth, coated in buff and deep blue. I lick the ouchie spot and the cord. More of the brown travels to my own leg and the evil squirrel stops twisting in her hands. The pain is now split between us— it will be easier for my Girlpup to do her thing.

All right.

Come on.

If I had fingers I'd tap them.

Hello! Isn't she supposed to have some instinct for this?

Karly takes a better hold of the squirrel's body with one hand and carefully touches the broken leg. The evil beast accepts it. I am taking a lot of the pain for the devil. Karly and I are still linked in our minds and I see distracting human color. She still isn't getting it. I think hard at her, showing her, in her own colors, glowing reds, whites, and pinks flowing from the Girlpup's hand to the squirrel. She nods at me and lets the colors spread over the ugly, dirty brown and flow around the cord between the squirrel and me. My skin feels hot and my own blue flows back to meet with her hand, cooling the harsh heat to a soft warmth. Now, I bite the strand holding me to the thing. It snaps back to the squirrel with a satisfying thwack. I feel Auntie Heather's look poking me. She knows I could have been nicer. Tough, she chose our patient. It won't even appreciate what we did.

Probably just throw twigs and acorns at us.

Evil things.

The bushy-tailed rat struggles against Karly's hand, scratches her, and high-tails it to the nearest tree.

Ungrateful monster.

I growl and bark, "You are dead if I ever see you again." Auntie Heather pokes me with another glare. I am not repentant; it scratched my Girlpup. I want it dead. Auntie Heather should be glad I am not turning the thing into worm food.

"Colors are energy. With George able to absorb some of the pain, it allows you to use other colors for their healing energy. That's why it's so important that you and George become a partnership. George sees energy differently than you do and you complement that." Auntie Heather riffles the fur behind my ears.

I am good.

I am good enough for a cookie. I lock eyes with hers and she laughs, gets up, and returns with cookies. "Karly, go in the kitchen and wash up. See if you can heal that scratch on your own. I think you'll find it much harder than working with others."

I consider following my quiet Girlpup to the house. The scent of cinnamon and beef make me drool. If Karly can't fix herself, I'll help. She needs the lesson; I need the cookie.

She better clean herself good. I can smell furry-tailed rat cooties on her. Yuck. I make a light woofing sound. Those cookies weren't any closer to my tummy than when they were in the kitchen. Auntie Heather tosses me a couple. I crunch them, happy to get the smell/taste of evil squirrel out of my mouth. I give her eyes guaranteed to get me another.

"Sorry George. You need to lose a pound or two. How will Karly learn if you can't keep up with her in the park?"

I blow out my lips at her. My body is as fit and fine as it can be.

"Let's go in, Karly must realize that she needs help by now." Aunt Heather retreats into the house and I follow before the door slams shut. Peeps forget about tails all the time.

Tailless monkeys.

"That was so cool, Aunt Heather. I've never seen anything like that from George's point of view," Karly says, standing by the sink. I'm glad the cat let her tongue go. She actually sounds impressed. "Why didn't we need water energy for big healing, though?" She looks down at her arm. "Maybe I need more water than what's coming from the faucet."

"Healing bones is normally tricky. Rupert is small and didn't need much color energy to repair his leg. Now, finish up, that scratch isn't getting any better. When you're done, would you like to work on trying to get more information about the bones?

"Well, yeah. But we don't have any of them. How can we do anything?"

Auntie Heather makes a shooing motion to both of us with her arms. "First, go to the bathroom and finish cleaning and healing."

We go obediently to the Peeps' bathroom. Karly is trying hard to bind the scratch—she never told me I had to leave her mind. I chuff out a little laugh. The scratch isn't very long or deep, but the Girlpup is having some trouble with it. It's good that she learns teamwork.

With a little push of color from me, the edges seal together. Yup, some things can't be learned in just one lesson. Then I remember—since I am still prowling around in her head—the smell of The Bad Thing in the woods. The mixed-up smell/tastes of skunk, cat-stink, gas, sulfur, and snakes fill our noses and cover our tongues. Maybe this time she'll get it.

"George, what are you doing? Why are you still in my mind and what's so stinky? Joey's socks smell better than that."

I try to show her what it means, but there's nothing to show. I don't know what The Bad Thing is. I know it's not a bushy-tailed rat. I shake in frustration. How can I tell her how important this is? Maybe Auntie Heather can help me.

Karly looks at her scratch and smiles. "You can keep your smelly thoughts to yourself, but thanks for helping me fix my scratch." She runs a finger over her smooth skin. "Wish I knew we could do that before. It would have saved a lot of bandages."

I couldn't tell her we couldn't have before. Karly smells different now and part of the scent is power. Is becoming a teenager making her powerful? I think about teenage dogs and sneeze. I have the scary vision of Karly humping everything in sight. I quickly leave Karly's mind, and hope she didn't see what I did.

My Girlpup doesn't say a word. Maybe she didn't get it. I whuff out a sigh of relief. I think she is right—I shouldn't wander in her mind.

Karly dries her hands on a towel. Silly, since she has perfectly good clothes for that. I take a moment to feel bad she was born without fur for protection. "'Kay, blockheaded freak, let's go see what Auntie Heather has next for us. Do you think we'll really figure out who the bones belonged to?"

I sneeze again. It wasn't who the bones belonged to when they were alive—it was who the bones belong to now that worries me. What was the Big Bad Thing that I can't recognize? My nose is the best, yet it let me down when I needed it the most. The most important thing is to protect Karly and Auntie Heather. I need more information. Playing with rocks and dead bones isn't going to do it for me. Karly finishes up and heads back to the gazebo, I follow behind, still trying to clear my traitorous nose.

Chapter Seven

We're in the park again. It's dryer than yesterday and a little cooler. Cooler is good for tracking, dry isn't.

Doesn't matter. I am a super sleuth with my nose. Karly is grumpy—she doesn't understand why we can't use more magic. Auntie Heather says magic is for special things. We shouldn't waste magic if we can use other methods. We're hunting The Bad Thing and my nose is magic enough. Peeps have bad tracking equipment. It's a good thing we're partners, they can't survive without us.

Auntie Heather snaps the leather leash on my collar so she won't get lost following me in the woods. I move too fast for Peeps, so Auntie slows me down so Karly can follow. I put my nose in the air and take a soft sniff. If The Bad Thing is around I don't want it to clog my nostrils with its stink. It's bad enough I still smell the evil squirrel.

The air is clear, so I set to work, nose to ground, ears shoveling scent, searching for the smell/taste of The Bad Thing. It doesn't take long.

I pull to it. It's the same spot I found earlier, surrounded by a ribbon of plastic. It smells like chemicals and will ruin my nose if I can't get away.

"That won't work. We can't cross the yellow tape, can we Auntie Heather?" Karly asks with dismay. Even I see the bright yellow of the tape. Is this how Peeps make pee-mail since they can't smell marking? It's yellow. It's about the right height for them. I can just go under.

Auntie Heather bends down and pats my head. "I bet there are more places that have that scent, aren't there? It's not here so there must be fresher scents somewhere. Can you find it?

Of course I can. I air-scent again, searching for The Bad Thing's gassulfurdrysnakecatstink tastesmell. I inhale and catch the oilytasting foulness. I wish I could spit.

One of my few design flaws.

I lean into the collar and pull into it, Auntie Heather a weight behind me. I tolerate her, but don't like it. I bay in frustration.

Hurry up.

"AroOOoooo!" I have it! I can find The Bad Thing now. Gah, I pull the leash out of Auntie Heather's hands. She and Karly have ears—they can hear my bay and follow that.

Free!

I run along the track, snorfling and breathing through my mouth, tasting the oil get stronger, the stink get stronger. My leash catches a branch and my collar chokes me. Karly calls me a blockhead and I am glad for once it's sort of true. My neck and head are about the same width.

I slip out of my collar and continue to follow my nose. There are scratchy sharp things under my feet and the ground is springy.

Really springy.

The trail twists and turns and I go up and up and…

"George! What are you doing up in that spruce tree? How'd you get up there?" My crazy Girlpup shouts at me.

As if.

Basset hounds are built for the ground, not the sky. The wind has picked up, blowing the scent all over the place. Karly and Auntie Heather are both yelling now. Since it's so important, I break my scent-connection and look for them.

There they are.

Below me.

Well, I think that's them, they look like ants. Wha—what am I doing in this tree? I panic and jump. I don't know what I am thinking, I am not a bird —my ears aren't meant for flying. Yikes! I make oofing sounds as branches brush by me, slowing me down. Finally, I land on the bottom branches and they spring slightly—just like jumping on a bed, not that I jump on beds. I'm a good boy.

I am good at planning, this one worked perfectly. I shake the needles off and trot over to my Pack.

"George, are you okay?" My Girlpup tries to scoop me up. My hind end dangles. I appreciate her attention, but my back doesn't feel great. Bouncing out of a tree will do that to a dog.

Auntie Heather rescues me from my partner's hug. "I think it might be better to practice your healing. His spine may be out of alignment." She turns to me. "George, what made you think you could climb the tree? Did your nose get ahead of your brain?"

It's obvious I can climb trees. As for my nose, it's always in front of my brain, right?

"Whine."

My back is not happy. If I am going to get The Bad Thing my body must in fighting shape. I lost to a tree, but it was a good lesson. I can only win against The Bad Thing if I use both my head and my nose.

My nose tells me there is something for me to find near my feet. I paw away the brown sharp things on the ground. The gassulfurdrysnakecatstink tastesmell is strong, pooled under a carpet of pokey things. A round shape with smaller round holes appears; The Bad Thing left a footprint. My fall must have covered it with, um, wait, I remember—needles. I lick my paw. There are sharp bits, sticky with sap, stuck in the pad. I bark, hold up my paw, and nose the print. I must look like a pointer. Ick, that's not a good look for me. My foot hurts when I put it down, so I plop my butt down. My back isn't happy with the curve I put into it by sitting.

Auntie Heather comes over and scrapes more of the sticky things away from the print. "It must have climbed the tree. I don't see any gouges or more prints here. Maybe he climbed it like George did." She pets my chest and continues to get rid of the needles. "Well, sort of like George. It never occurred to me that a spruce tree was like a spiral staircase, at least to a dog. Anyway, good job, boy, but next time call us. You can tree your quarry without climbing for it. Karly, let's fix your familiar and see what else he can find."

"Can I do it without him? I mean, before it took both of us," my Girlpup asks. I can feel her lack of confidence. If I felt better I would snuggle with her, instead, I warble encouragement.

"He sounds like he has a tummy ache," my brilliant Girlpup tells Auntie Heather. Where did she get that idea? I shake my head and hold out my foot.

Auntie Heather takes my paw and runs her hand over the pads. "This doesn't need healing, just a little cleaning." She pulls out the needles and tries to get the sticky stuff off. "When we get back I'll put some olive oil on this. It works well for cutting through sap. He's going to pick up more debris. Just like his paws have double-sided tape on them. Nothing to do about it now."

I tilt my head and gaze into her eyes. It feels much better without sharp things in between my toes. I take a swipe at my paw with my tongue and use my teeth to pull off some of the stickysweetpiney goo. I am about to swallow it when Auntie Heather tells me to drop it. I give her my best begging eyes.

Please?

She looks serious and I drop it at her feet. Mousefleas. It might be good —like sidewalk gum.

"So do I heal him the same way we did Rupert?" Karly has her hands on my spine. She stops when I wince at a sore spot. "It's really hot here."

Auntie Heather moves Karly's hand from my back and gently touches the hot spot. "He has a strain. Normally I'd just give him some white willow, but since we're still going to hunt, let's give him a little boost. If one or both of you get hurt, the healing method is similar to what you did earlier. It'll be quicker if I do it this time, though. Roque?"

My buddy clatters down a tree just to the right of us. He's showing off. He can be as silent as a can of dog food. I don't even smell him. He's very good at camouflage and has offered to teach me, though I won't be hiding in trees anytime soon.

Maybe under.

Auntie Heather keeps her hand on my back, slowly massaging the area. Roque puts his little hands on top of hers and I feelsmell/taste blue flowers, sweet and warm in the sun.

I crane my neck to see better and watch the glow surround my back and their hands. The hurt melts away and I feel like I had a nap and water, and am ready to rock and roll.

Woot!

Auntie Heather and Roquefort have healed me in the past and it's always wonderful. They lift their hands away from me, Auntie Heather strokes me, Roquefort sniffs my ears, and I slurp his face. He chatters at me, only a little put out by my gratitude. Raccoons don't understand doggy kisses, but he's getting better at accepting my gestures of love.

Roquefort clambers back up a tree and disappears into the leaves. Auntie Heather finds the leash and collar and puts it back on. "George, I'm not as young as I used to be, so take pity. I understand the power of smell/taste, but restrain yourself so we don't have to heal me."

I nod. A good dog doesn't deliberately hurt his Peep. I wait until she stands up and raise my head to catch air scent. There's nothing except what's leading from the footprint, so I return and follow the drying scent. My mouth is getting dry from being open gathering the smell/taste. I never remember how thirsty I get tracking. Auntie Heather shakes her head and reaches into the bag she has on her back. She pulls out a water bottle, twists off the cap, and pours it slowly into my cheek so I don't choke. It's a little warm, but it tastes wonderful.

"Sorry, George, I forgot, too. Do you want to rest or go home?"

I snort when I am done and do the shake business, getting everything into place. The fog around my nose blows away and smell/tastes rush in more clearly. I am ready and put my super nose back on the trail.

Weird.

Sometimes, I catch it above the floor of the woods, and sometimes it's buried under the leaves and needles. It goes around trees and sometimes up them. I want to climb again.

Auntie Heather gives a gentle tug on the leash. "Four on the floor, George."

As if.

I'm an automatic. 'Kay, so my nose is on automatic. I put it back on the ground and stay with the ground scent. Why does the scent jump around so much? I am a dog on a mission and follow the smell/taste of gassulfurdrysnakecatstink, even though I wish it wasn't getting stronger. That's good—it means I am getting closer. It's bad because I want to toss my cookies.

My right rear foot stumbles over a branch. Another branch grabs my left front. What the…The scent is very strong here, but it keeps going off to the left. I try to escape the trap. The more I struggle, the more I get myself in a tangle. To top it off, Auntie Heather is holding the leash too tight. What's wrong with her, she knows better.

Cough. Gack.

"Quit struggling George. There's a big hole under those branches and if you keep moving forward you're going to fall in."

I let Auntie Heather pull me out of the snarl of branches like a fish.

How embarrassing.

I'm the one supposed to protect her. Karly kneels next to me and runs her hands over me. She hits my tickle spot and my hind leg shakes. Hee. Stop it now, work to do.

Karly moves her hand away from the spot and gives me a final scritch. "You're okay." She gasps as she points to the hole. "Auntie Heather, what is that?"

Auntie Heather pulls a few more branches away from the hole and we all look in. It's deep. I can't see anything. The smell/taste is hot and feels thick in my mouth. I sneeze to clear it away.

Doesn't help.

Gack.

"George, is anything in there?" Auntie Heather bends to stroke my ears.

Well, yes. There are things in there. Metal things. Wood things. Plate things. Bone things. Peep bones.

I am not going in there, even though there's no one home. I don't like to see Peep bones without the bodies that pet and give food. My tail swishes low and I back up.

Nope. Not going, and nothing can make me. I brace my feet.

Auntie Heather cocks her head at me. "Fine. We won't go in there yet." She turns to my panting, but otherwise very quiet, Girlpup. "I don't think anything's in there now." Auntie Heather sniffs and wrinkles her nose. "Do you smell anything?"

Finally! Someone is using her nose.

Head.

Same difference.

"Yeah, that's the same horrible stink that George made me smell when I was cleaning up. What is it? He sure seems to like it and wanted to share." My Girlpup shudders. Usually I'd disagree about a scent being bad, but I agree with her.

Auntie Heather shakes her head and stares at Karly hard. "You need to pay attention to him. When did he share it with you?"

My Girlpup squirms and traces a line in the needles with her shoe. "He shared it with me when we first found the shredded tree. I thought it was just another smelly scent he wanted to share because he thought it was good. How was I supposed to know he wanted me to know it was whatever the thing is?"

"Context, Karly. You were near a site with fresh signs. George can't use words—you're aware of that. When he opens the link try to figure out why, don't just make a snap judgment. Oh, and I forgot to ask if you started a computer search?"

"Not really. It was getting late."

"Well, then it isn't so important, but you may have missed an important and timely clue. You can describe the smell when you do your search." Auntie Heather gathered the branches and covered the hole again. "I'd rather not do this, something might fall in. I'm just worried that whatever dug this out will come back and find it disturbed. If we can smell it, it could smell us."

"Aren't you going to tell the police?" Karly looked confused—not that it's unusual. She really needs to pay attention to me, like Auntie Heather says. I can answer most of her questions. We don't need the Badge Dude.

Um.

Well, maybe. He does have guns. Guns might be useful.

"This isn't a mundane creature. There's something mystical out there and we're far better equipped than they are. Let's continue sleuthing until we find out more information. Perhaps I'm wrong. Still, those bones aren't fresh so I don't think it will hurt to spend a couple more days looking for answers."

I know it isn't a common variety skunk. Why don't they ask me anything? Like, will it come back? Should they make a circle of protection to keep other things from falling in the hole? The branches cover it too well. I am afraid animals and Peeps can fall in and get hurt.

Or eaten by The Bad Thing if it comes back.

Auntie Heather nods—she understands my thoughts. I feel warm and snuggly. It's good to have someone who gets me without my having to trip them to get their attention.

"Help me construct a circle around the nest. We need to make sure nothing finds it and tumbles in by accident. If we construct this right, we'll be able to tell if the creature tries to cross the circle." Auntie Heather reaches into the bag she always carries on her back and pulls out a small mesh pouch with sweet smelltasting herbs. I paw her to let me sniff and lick the bundle.

"Sorry George, not for you and dog spit isn't going to make it work any better. Karly, cup your left hand." Auntie Heather sprinkles some of the mixture into my Girlpup's hand. I almost swoon, it smell/tastes so good. It wouldn't protect against me.

"It's made with kitchen herbs with a sprinkling of sea salt. The recipe is in your many-times great-grandmother Leah's cookbook." Auntie Heather takes position on the edge of the nest.

"I'm going to walk in a circle around the hole and you're going to follow, sprinkling the mixture behind you. As you walk, I want you to picture a wall of bright light rising up behind you. George is closest to the wild energy of the woods and can cement the circle into place, a sort of 'No Trespassing' sign. The best analogy I can come up with is we're making a fishnet, weaving the energy of the crystals with the strength in the herbs."

In other words, I get to pee on the corners.

If circles had corners. Well, that's my addition. I am accepted as a natural part of the woods, not like a Peep.

Auntie Heather scowls at me. "The plants and animals will recognize this is a power circle and lend their own energy to prevent anything from crossing the circle without that addition. Just add your energy to Karly's please."

Personally, I think pee-mail will work better.

Roquefort comes out of the trees and follows me. He might be better at collecting the wild energies, but I'll never tell him. He's already got a big head.

Not like me.

He raises his masked face to me and chitters. I hate it when he laughs at me.

We finish with the circle and it shimmers like heat on a road when it's very hot.

Beautiful.

Mmm, it smells nummy.

Auntie Heather pulls out a bell on a chain around her neck and rings it. Bands of sound hit the shimmer and stop. The circle works. "I think that's enough for today, you look exhausted. You've done more magic than we normally do in a week. I'll take you home. I bet you have schoolwork and if you have time…" Auntie Heather gives her the 'adult' eye. "You can start a computer search for missing persons. Do your homework first."

Karly does look like something the cat coughed up. I nudge her ankle and share a little of the energy that surrounds me. She used too much to make the circle, but she'll learn. My Girlpup looks down and smiles at me. Good, she recognized what I did. Oh yeah, she'll learn. I am a good teacher. We follow Auntie Heather out of the woods to go home to my supper dish.

Chapter Eight

I fell asleep on Karly's foot last night, so I don't know how much time she put in on her re-search. We didn't go back in the woods to search again, so how the computer can help her search is beyond me. I woke up under the computer desk listening to her grumble about homework taking too much time. Dogs have it good, no homework, no leaving our dens to work. Silly Peeps work too hard. There's not enough time for them to take naps, rub our bellies, or feed us. They never feed us. I fall back asleep until my tummy alarm goes off.

I crawl out from under the desk and trot to Karly's bed. I snuffle in her ear—the only way to get her attention since I'm not allowed on the bed. No one said I couldn't put my front paws up. I lick her nose. Wake up. *Wakeup*, Girlpup, I haven't eaten anything in months. I am going to die of starvation if I don't get breakfast. Mmm, breakfast. I drool.

On her face.

If you don't get up you're going to have wet shoes.

And a puppy present near the door.

It'll be your fault, too.

Karly stretches and bats my head away. Hey, don't do that. I bonk her with my muzzle and sit next to the bed.

Hurry up Girlpup.

It's not like you don't know the drill—we do this every morning.

"Mmmmf. George, cut it out. It's a vacation day; I get to sleep in during spring break." She rolls away from me, hiding her head under a pillow.

What is this vacation stuff? It's a day. Days start with my breakfast and a walk. I wuffle. She pulls the covers up. I yap. She digs in deeper. I bark. She doesn't move. I go to the foot of the bed, get a good mouthful of covers, and pull. I keep pulling backward until I hit the closet behind me. I pull until all the covers are on the floor. A stuffie falls to the floor. When I was a pup I thought it was mine and nibbled a little hole in its wing. She didn't share and took it back. It's always out of my reach now. It's just a stupid lizard thing with wings.

"*George!*" Karly's head pops up over the edge of the bed. She isn't happy. She usually wakes up grumpy. I thump my tail and give her my best eyes. They are melting eyes that show her how much I love her and how much I need to eat.

She moans, rubs her eyes, and pulls her hands through her fur. It's standing up in funny points. Dogs never wake up frazzled. We are predators, always aware of our surroundings. We are wolves that found better living arrangements. Though right now, I don't think much of them. I bark and bounce in front of the door. Hurry up, Karly! I am going to melt into skin and bones. My bladder is going to burst. I don't know which is more important to deal with first.

Karly stretches her arms high above her head and pulls the blankets back. "'Kay blockheaded freak, give me a minute and I'll take you outside to potty."

I sit and stare at her.

Move it.

Cover your Chinese Crested pink skin.

Hurryhurryhurry! I do my potty dance by the door.

"Oh for the love of peanut butter. I'm going as fast as I can." Karly pulls on some little things and then a shirt and jeans. Though why jeans are named after a friend of hers is weird. "Let's go outside."

She opens the door out of the bedroom and I make a mad dash to the door that goes outside.

"Hang on, you know the score," Karly grabs her leash and clips it to my collar. "Stop pulling, you aren't going to burst."

Easy for her to say.

"Hey, I haven't even gone to the bathroom yet." She grumbled, "And Joey is probably using up all the hot water."

"Karly? I didn't realize you were awake. I'll have pancakes ready for you when you get back. Don't dawdle." I can smell the breakfast Packmom is making. Guess I'll only check the pee-mail on our block.

Karly and I make it out just in time. I sniff the base of the big tree by the street, checking for anything new.

Nothing much.

I continue to check each tree, finding out which of my friends were out already today.

Not too many.

So much nothing.

"George, would you hurry up and potty already? I have to go, too, and besides, we have a ton to do today."

Like what? Something more important than checking today's pee-mail? You spend enough time on the Internet looking at yours. You're just jealous because you can't mark a tree.

What's that?

We pass a house with a big yard surrounded by a chain link fence. There are lots of dogs yapping, playing tug of war, or jumping over sticks hanging between two others. I don't remember ever seeing this before. I pull Karly to the fence and sit.

One dog is running with her partner. The partner is lazy, just making loops around the big things scattered around the yard. The black and white border collie is hollering sharp yaps as she runs through tunnels, jumps over sticks, climbs up wooden hills. I turn my head and look at Karly. We could do that. I could teach her teamwork doing this. What is this?

Karly's eyes dart from the yard to me. "George, not going to happen. You couldn't climb any of that stuff much less jump those jumps. You are the least agile animal that ever walked on four paws."

What the...That's just rude. I could do it. A small wiener dog is next up. It leaps over very low jumps, climbs up the hill, and races up through a tunnel. It really looks like fun. By the end, though, the little guy is panting his heart out and breathing hard. Um. I didn't realize it was that much work. I am plenty agile; I just don't see the point of running if there isn't a rabbit involved. Besides, Karly and I are a team. No way is she leading me in loops.

This is stupid.

I bite the leash and pull Karly to a line of trees next to the road. I finish my business and kick some grass and dirt over it. My Girlpup cleans up my mess like a good Peep, and we head home for breakfast. I am going to die of starvation if we don't get back now. Why are we still here?

* * * *

"Pancakes are on the table," my Packmom, Doreen, shouts from the kitchen. "There's one for George in his bowl, mixed in with his kibble."

"Moooom. I want another one," The Creep whines. This Boypup needs to learn how to whine properly. I whine to show him the proper way. Well, I want my food too.

Karly snaps off her leash and hangs it on the peg next to the door. I shake my fur to settle everything back into place. She mussed up my ears a little. "Mom, Auntie Heather says that George needs to lose a couple of pounds. *No pancakes!*"

What? I race to the kitchen before Packmom takes them away. I earned those pancakes with my nice walk and proper pottying.

"He can start his diet tonight. I'd have to waste all this food, the pancakes are stirred in," my beloved Packmom tells my stingy Girlpup. "Joey, I'll make you some more after I'm done with mine. Karly, I'll just give George less food from here on. I think some green beans and pumpkin will keep his tummy full."

"As if. The dog is a walking stomach."

Well, not exactly, but food is very important to keep my nose working properly.

Karly takes her seat at the table and Packmom puts a plate in front of her. I sit on her foot and wag my tail.

My turn.

"If you move off my foot, I can get your food."

Oh, right.

"So, did you find out anything about the bones you found?" My Packmom puts a bowl in front of my nose. It smell/tastes wonderful in my nose—mapleburntegghotflourticklecinnamonmaple mixed with fishcoldcrunch kibble. I take my first bite, and then really chow down. My bowl is empty! Someone stole my food. Aaaaagh! Packmom! Packmom, it's empty, I am starving, and my food is all gone.

Burp.

Excuse me.

Karly narrows her eyes at me and finishes chewing before she turns to Packmom. "I'm not sure. George found a bunch of junk that Auntie Heather thought might be important. He also found some weird tracks, and trees that have shredded bark. I started to do a search last night, but since someone says…" Karly's voice trails off while she gives Packmom a glare before she continues, "…I'm not allowed to use the computer until my homework is done, I didn't get to."

"So your homework is done? Do you want me to go over it with you?"

"No, that's 'kay, homework was easy. After breakfast I want to see if I can find anything about the bones or whatever is out there." Karly shovels more breakfast in her mouth, almost as fast as I can.

Packmom pulls a chair out and sits next to Karly. "Easy. It's Sunday, you aren't late, and you can enjoy your breakfast." She takes a bite of pancake off a plate that was magically already there. Food is never magically there in my bowl. I sit pretty, but she doesn't share. "I'd rather you go outside today. It's too pretty a day to waste it inside. Why don't you see if Heather needs you for something."

I agree with Packmom.

The Creep has to break in. "I want to go, too. Please, can I go?"

Karly talks through a mouthful of pancake as she glares at The Creep. "She needs me to do a computer search."

"Which you can do tonight. When you're finished it's your turn to do the dishes, and then out you go. Just let me know before you go, 'kay? Oh, and avoid the woods until they catch whatever shredded the trees. Even if it doesn't have anything to do with the old bones I'd feel more comfortable if you stayed away. Let the police and your aunt—since I can't imagine her not getting involved—deal with it. Joey, the garden needs weeding. There are strawberries and peas ready for picking. You can help me. When your father gets back from the lumberyard he's going to work on the new shed. He mentioned he needed your help."

The Creep bounces in his seat. His plate falls to the floor without breaking. I am on it like a flash and clean it better than the dishwasher will ever do.

"Mooooom!" The Creep still doesn't get how to whine. I wince at his high pitch. This Boypup better mature soon.

"Pick it up and rinse it off. You can have one of my pancakes, I'm getting full."

Impossible.

Well, maybe Packmom has another extra. I walk over to her chair and rest my head on her lap. Please? I bat my eyelashes. Cruel Peep, she just laughs.

"I'm done. May I be excused?" I know Karly says this automatically. It just seems strange she would want to be excused from eating more. Peeps seldom made sense.

Karly's leash is on the floor. My Girlpup will never find it there, so I drag it to her. It's time to go see Auntie Heather. I hope she's planning to head back to the park. That Bad Thing is on the loose and the Badge Dude isn't going to find it without my nose.

"Mom, why can't I go with Karly?"

"If you do the dishes for her, I'm sure she'll be glad to have you tag along." Packmom winks at Karly, who is rigid at her seat. Yeah, I don't want him along, either.

"No. I don't really want to go. Guess I'll wait for Dad." Joey takes a big gulp of juice and races out the door, sticking out his tongue at Karly as he passes her.

Karly sighs dramatically, collects the dishes, and washes them.

Yawn.

This is taking her forever. The world could end before she finishes. I have to eat before the world ends.

Karly's shout wakes me up. When did I fall asleep? "Mom, I'm going to Auntie Heather's now."

"You don't have to shout. Try to be home for dinner, it'd be nice to have the whole family together for a change."

"I'll try. Anything you want from Auntie Heather?" Karly picks up her backpack and her leash.

"Go on, shoo, go learn magic from your aunt. When you get home I'll teach you some magic." Packmom uses her hands like she's pushing Karly out the door.

"I thought you didn't know any."

"I know the magic of folding fitted sheets."

Karly rolls her eyes, clips her leash to my collar, and tugs me out the door. Gagging, I follow.

Chapter Nine

I snoof around Auntie Heather's kitchen. Roquefort must've been in, there isn't even a crumb and Auntie Heather usually leaves plenty on the floor.

"I froze some nonfat yogurt for you, George, and there are plenty of baby carrots for your snack later."

I give her puppy eyes. She rolls hers.

"You just had breakfast."

Harumph.

"So what's up for today?" Karly asks as she steals a Snickerdoodle cookie from the counter. Auntie Heather doesn't say a word about the obvious theft. This is so unfair.

"I think we need to go back to the hole with some equipment. My bag is filled with candles, crystals, oils, and herbs. Oh, and your grandmother's silver bell, its sound is sweeter and the power stronger than my little brass one, and a rope ladder of course. I also want to take some pictures. Did you find anything on the Internet?"

Karly's eyes dropped to the ground. "Mom wanted me to get my homework out of the way. I told her it was vacation, but..."

"Oh, I didn't think. Of course you did." Auntie Heather made a clucking sound with her mouth. She sounds like a chicken I heard at the fair when Karly took me to a 4-H thing. "I agree with your mom, it's better to get it over with. The computer is such a time suck, isn't it? I did a little research of my own, using some old books my grandmother, your great-grandmother, stored in the attic. Our many-times great-grandparents wrote some of them. I thought I saw something familiar about the paw print."

"What? What is it?" If Karly could explode, she would. She's quivering like a pointer on a bird. Course, I want to know, too. I am just too cool to quiver. Drooling isn't excitement. I shuffle closer to Auntie. What is The Bad Thing and why doesn't it take a bath? It surprises me the Badge Dude couldn't smell it.

Auntie Heather carries a book as long as my front leg and about as wide, big, and heavy looking. I try to stand on my hind legs to sniff it.

"George, off. This is too fragile for you to paw. Come over here, Karly, where the light's better."

Karly obediently follows Auntie Heather to a window seat in the front room. I beat them there and jump up onto it, starting to make my three turns. It's nice to nap in the sun.

Auntie Heather sighs. "George, I know you think this is your spot, but we need to use it for a bit. Move your butt." She gives me a soft shove and I ooze to the floor.

Fine.

It's too hot in the window anyway.

She opens the book to a spot marked by a ribbon. There is a drawing of a four-legged thing. I sit straight and crane my neck to see the picture better. Whoa, that is one ugly creature.

"It's green? And are those scales with fur? What are those spikes on its back and head? I don't get it. Are you sure this picture isn't from a great-relative's nightmare? Maybe it's a dinosaur? Except they're extinct." Karly sounds as confused as I feel. "Wow, look at the claws on it. It sort of looks like an elephant without a trunk. Are those more claws on its back and tail? No way is that real."

"I believe it's quite real." Auntie Heather smiles. "It's too old to have been changed with a computer program."

"What is it then? I don't think I've ever seen anything like that at the zoo."

The zoo won't let me in, but I can't imagine they'd have anything so stinky there.

Auntie Heather looks at me. "They have skunks."

How does she do that so easily? I have to bang on Karly's mental shields to get her to let me in. Humph. I scootch as close as I can to the book, rest my head on the bench, and sneeze. I agree with Karly—nothing looks like that. Nothing smells like that, either.

Not even those stripey kitties.

"It's called a Hodag. They're very rare creatures, a link between dinosaurs and mammals," Auntie Heather uses a finger to trace what she's reading.

Never understood why Peeps insist on writing when scent and markings give a more complete picture. I know it's a dinosaur-mammal. What's a dinosaur-mammal? Can I eat it?

Auntie Heather pushes my head away before a string of drool drops on her book.

Karly shakes her head. "No, Aunt Heather." She points to the black squiggles. "According to this it was a prank. There isn't any such thing as a Hodag. Um, except for the school mascot in Rhinelander, Wisconsin. "

"Keep reading. After all, some people don't think there is any such thing as magic. And yet…"

How can anyone not believe in magic? They must ignore the changing seasons and life.

Sheesh.

Peeps can be blind.

"George, it's that disbelief that we can use to hide things in plain sight. Well, Karly, what do you see now?"

The book is too bulky for Karly to lift so she gets closer, with her nose nearly pressed to the page. "The words are swirling around. I can hardly make it out. Um, stop it." She shakes the book. "Stop moving. Stupid words. 'Kay. The paragraph is different now." If she doesn't close her mouth a fly is going to land in it.

"You need to remember that magic requires belief. You accepted what you read the first time. Next time, ask the book if it has anything else to share before you close it."

Makes sense. If the Peeps have to store their information, I wish their books would talk to me. Too hard to read and turn pages with my nose—they get all gooey and stick together. Books aren't made very well.

Karly's jaw opened and she looked up at Auntie. "They're preserved by witches because they're lucky? Why would we preserve monsters that eat humans?"

That's a good question. The only things that should be eaten are bacon, steak, chicken nuggets, hamburger, and fish.

Not Peeps.

"We really don't know that those people were killed, much less eaten, by the Hodag. It's a good puzzle. Puzzle or not, from now on, the only time you go into the woods is with me. Is that clear?"

Karly carefully puts the book back on the seat. "Yes, Auntie Heather. I don't think I want to meet the Hodag by myself." She glances down at me. "Mr. Short Legs wouldn't be much help if a dinosaur tried to kill us."

I harumph. Auntie Heather shakes her head and rolls her eyes. "Karly, the Hodag isn't a monster. I bet they're the basis for dragon stories." She points to the picture in the book. "This looks a lot like the Chinese dragon and some of the dragon figurines you collect, doesn't it?"

Karly looks at the picture again, tracing the outline of the Hodag Bad Thing with her finger. I admit, those things would come in handy sometimes. "Maybe. A little. An ugly dragon maybe."

I lift up a little and sniff the picture before Auntie Heather can stop me. It's very ugly and it doesn't smell like gassulfurdrysnakecatstink.

Books are silly—they don't have the right information. This one smells like old paper, ink, and, hmmm, is that cake batter? I lift up a little again and try to lick the page. Auntie Heather pulls me back with my collar. Curses, foiled again. My hero, Snoopy, used to say that in the comics Karly sometimes reads to me.

"This is a cook book, George. It has recipes in it, and nothing for you to eat, or to sample," Auntie Heather says before she lets go of my collar.

That's totally unfair, I might add. I never grab a Peep by their shirt collars.

Not since puppyhood, anyway.

Auntie Heather picks up a bag that smells yummy. I wag my tail. She doesn't even notice I exist. "It's for lunch. You can wait. I think we should go back out to the park and see if anything tripped the circle. Now that we know what we might be looking for it should be easier to find more clues. If it's really like a dragon, then that nest we found might be its treasure trove."

Why would it be any easier than it was when I used my nose?

"Wouldn't there be fire marks on the trees? Don't dragons breathe fire?" Karly doesn't sound any more convinced than I am.

Auntie Heather taps on a small picture. "Maybe this one doesn't breathe fire. However, do you see the paw prints? Nearly perfectly round with peg-like claw marks."

"That doesn't explain why we only see one print on the ground and the shredded bark." My Girlpup reaches down and scratches behind my ears. She knows the itchiest spots and I rub my head closer into her hand.

"OooOOoooo."

Good Girlpup. I moan and my leg shakes.

How embarrassing.

Auntie Heather flips a few more pages. "This might be the answer." She traces another picture. "It looks like they use only their rear leg to pogo up trees. If they don't get up as far as they want they slide down the trunk."

Or, they are scent marking. I think that makes better sense. Once again, the Peeps don't remember they have noses.

"Auntie Heather, this is silly. Everyone knows that dragons breathe fire and fly. They don't pogo into trees hoping to land where they want and sliding down if they don't. What kind of potion was great-great-great-great whatever making before she painted these pages?" Karly giggles. I'd laugh, too, except I don't think this is funny. It's a Bad Thing that munched on Peeps bones.

"Have you ever seen a Hodag or a dragon?" Auntie Heather looks serious, I can tell by the crinkles in her forehead. They are very attractive. "Why thank you, George."

It's no wonder that Karly hates me wandering in her mind without permission.

"No, of course not. No one has ever seen them. The book said the Hodag was supposed to be a prank."

Auntie Heather checks out her watch. "Well, only one way to find out. Let's go to the park. Let's walk, it's too nice a day to drive. Leash up."

Karly searches for her leash. In the meantime, I grab it off the porch where she dropped it and drop it at her feet. She needs to clip it to the handle. It would make a pretty collar and she wouldn't lose it.

Auntie Heather smiled at me. Yep, it isn't quite as much fun when someone else tiptoes through my mind. "That's not a bad idea. Karly, the next time you remove the leash, fasten the clasp to the handle and hang it around your neck. It'll save you a lot of time if you didn't have to search for your leash all the time."

Did I mention that Auntie Heather is a smart Peep?

Karly rolls her eyes and clips the leash on. I hope I don't have to drag her to the park—she's so slow sometimes. We leave and Auntie Heather locks her house.

Not good if someone steals the fridge.

The sidewalk is hot and I pull to the grass. Karly tries to yank me back, but I am strong and low. No way am I walking on a hot sidewalk. I put my nose down and snuffle deeply, checking my pee-mail. Hm, the furball twins are out today. The scent is fresh and I follow it to several poles and trees. I lift my leg on all of them to tell my friends and strangers I was here.

Ah, there they are. "Aroo," I call out. My tail spins on its own. They are silly looking—little like puppies, buff colored and hairy.

Short noses.

Not proper.

Except some dogs long ago decided they liked to be babied by their Peeps. Whatever works.

Their Packpeeps call them Tommy and Tuffy. They don't have a good name like mine. They smell the chemicalsweet of their Peeps. I think they sit on their Peeps' laps.

A lot.

I hope someday that Karly will tell me why Peeps have to put stinky chemicals on their bodies. They smell much better without it. Peeps should always smell like they do after fishing or hunting.

The fur balls pull their Packpeep's leashes trying to reach me. Their yips of greeting make me feel good. It's nice to have friends. I pull Karly over. We greet each other nose to butt. Yup, definitely Tommy and Tuffy, unless they exchanged rear ends.

Hey, it could happen.

Karly and Auntie Heather don't do it right. They both say "hello" to Tommy and Tuffy's Peep and make noise.

I take a closer sniff of Tommy's rear and flare my nostrils. Gassulfurdrysnakecatstink smell/taste is tangled in his fur. Campfire, like the ones Packdad makes for s'mores? I only get graham crackers and marshmallow.

No.

No s'mores' smell/taste. There is also the sweetgreenmustysoil smell/taste of the park. I sniff Tuffy, moving around to his mouth. He carries the same scent plus pee and dead mouse.

Lucky Tuffy.

Had they seen The Bad Thing?

We face each other. Both Tommy and Tuffy yawn and their eyes are wide, showing whites. They are afraid. I show them it's okay by licking my lips. But, is it? Tuffy spins, growls, paws the ground, and yips. There was something. They could have fought it, but it was gone.

I am glad they didn't run into The Bad Thing. I lick my lips again. I slurp their muzzles and "aroo" to them. Leave it to me—I am a great hunting dog. I trundle over to their Peep and lick her ankle, looking back to the fur balls. They dance back to their Packmate and paw and jump on her. They understand they must protect her. I lick Tuffy's side and sneeze to let them know they have to stay out of the park.

Doggy language is clear as glass.

Positive they know their job, I trundle back to Karly. She is telling their Packmate the same thing.

I pull my Girlpup and gargle to Auntie Heather. Time to gogogo! Now! The Bad Thing is in the park.

Must catch it!

Need to find the campfire, too.

"Looks like George is on a mission," Tommy and Tuffy's Peep says, holding her own Pack back. They want to go home. "Are you going to the demonstration this early?"

"Oh no! Please tell me that isn't today," Auntie Heather groans.

The Peep looks at the band on her wrist. "In about an hour. Most of the witches from the area and neighbors are coming. I thought you were involved with putting this together." She has a beautiful crease in her forehead. It's sad that it means the Peeps are confused. "Oh and be careful. Someone set small fires in the wooded part of the park. I'm afraid they might blame us for it."

"I was," Auntie Heather mumbles under her breath. "I guess I forgot what day it was. Of course we'll be there, thanks for reminding me. Wouldn't look good to miss my own party." She begins to smell like fearsweat. It isn't a good time for other Peeps in the woods part of the park. "Thanks for warning me about the fires. That's awful."

"Isn't it? I wonder who did it. Maybe it was the contractor, to scare us away. Well, don't get too lost in your plant collecting. The bulldozers are scheduled to start taking down trees and we need to block them from the park entrance. Besides, I haven't heard anything about the police finding out where those old bones George found came from. I'm sure it's safe—" I growl and she looks down at me. I smile back at her. "—Um, I'm sure it's safe, they were old bones after all, but still. Oh, and I need to have a wart looked after. Maybe tomorrow?"

Auntie Heather agrees and the Peeps say their goodbyes. I wag my tail at the fluff balls and they wag back. Enough with this, time to gogogo. I stomp my paws. "Arrrufaroo!"

"Guess we gotta go," Karly tells the small Pack.

Smart Karly.

If I had a treat, I'd give it to her. I am proud of her. She's learning my language so well. I know she's trainable.

Just a little stubborn.

Chapter Ten

I smell/taste The Bad Thing right away. Woods usually suck scent in. This is rolling over the parking lot like fog, and onto the big machines. I don't like the equipment and wish they were gone, but I feel bad they have the foggy stuff touching them. I put my nose down on the pavement. It smell/tastes like dead tree smoke and burnt green leaves.

Not a typical smell/taste for the woods.

There is a gob of gum on the ground. I lick it and try to pull it up. Karly jerks me back.

Spoil sport.

Auntie Heather's shoes squeak a little on the pavement. She points to a big herd of Peeps standing near the big machines. "They came early. I hope no one decides to follow us."

"Can't we dull our edges so no one can see us?" Karly always wants a chance to use her magic craft.

"That usually only works if no one saw us. Since Belinda, who is a busybody witch, is walking this way we've already been spotted. Let's go into the woods before she gets here and you can try your spell. If it doesn't work we'll have to wait until after the demonstration."

I lead Karly to the top of the trail and pull her behind some bushes. Auntie Heather's shoes stop squeaking, but something in her backpack tinkclinks. Is it a supper bowl? She puts a hand behind her and pulls out a pouch of herbs.

Of course it's not. I tell my tummy that we are still working. It rumbles back at me. Auntie Heather and Karly glare at me. I sit and look around.

It's a woods.

Yep.

"This is from the batch you made. It's getting a bit old, but I think it will still work."

Karly takes the pouch from Auntie Heather. The pouch looks like a tea bag, but it smell/tastes like dust, mold, and rotting things. I like it and try to take a lick. Karly holds it out of my reach. She shakes some into her hand and poofs it with some words and her breath into the air. She doesn't need the words. I'll show her how when she is more willing to share our minds. It lands on my coat. My nose tickles and "achooh, choo," I sneeze. More of it swirls around, shiny dust in the sun. Magic takes shape around us.

Roquefort tags my butt; I jump straight up. Even if the woods weren't dead he would've caught me. I glare at him and plot ways of getting even.

"Oh good, you're here. Did you find anything?" Auntie Heather pets her familiar and I am a little jealous. I shake off the jealousy. Karly is mine, not Auntie Heather.

"Do they allow grilling now?" Karly looks around. "The herbs shouldn't smell like smoke, should they?" She scrunches her face and takes a deep breath. Peeps try so hard. She could ask me where the smell/taste is coming from.

"That isn't coming from my herbs. That must be from the fires that were set. Did the spell work?" Now she looks at her hands and feet.

All sparkly.

I bend around and look at my glossy, sleek coat. It's all sparkly, too. Funny that sparkles dull us so we blend into the background. Unless someone knows we're here. Would they see our sparkles? I crinkle my nose. I am handsome enough without sparklies.

"Heather? Are you here? Heather?" Auntie Heather's friend's shout broke the quiet.

Huh, that's weird. I hadn't noticed how quiet it is. The creatures aren't talking.

No evil squirrel taunts, no angry birds squawking at me. Not even any stinging bugs herding me out because they think I don't belong here. Hah, I am a great hunter. They're afraid of me.

When they are here.

Where are they?

"I could have sworn I saw her," the friend murmurs as she moves back to the parking lot. Mission accomplished. I sneeze again and move out of the sparkly cloud.

"Let's go before someone else decides they want to take a hike. I want to at least check out the pit," Auntie Heather tells us as she pushes through the plants and shrubs. I would like to mark them, but she turns her head and shakes it. "No." Sigh. 'Kay. Not now, anyway.

I drag my Karly to the pit. As we get closer the trees show burn marks. The worst are closest to the hole—shredded bark is burned black. Someone had a bad night. My nose drips from the smell of The Bad Thing mixed with charred wood. I like campfires. I don't like trees hurt for no reason. If it wanted to mark its territory it should leave pee-mail, not hurt defenseless plant things.

"George, wait, stop. George, I'm going to trip. GEORGE!" my paw-disadvantaged Girlpup pants out. I slow down.

A little.

Auntie Heather keeps up with me, her bag rustling and she pulls out a bell.

Not a supper dish.

Darn.

The soft tinkclinks of the bell calls out like a bird. Bird? I like to chase birds. I look for them. No, all the birds are gone. The Bad Thing needs to be gone, not my birds. The Bad Thing can keep the squirrels.

We reach the pit. Auntie Heather digs out the pretty bell and rings it. The sound bounces off the circle and chimes back to us. The circle is still up. The trees and bushes around the hole are trash. Bark, branches, and leaves are ripped to shreds and burned to dark bits—not a good smell/taste. I cough it back off my tongue. Charcoal doesn't taste good even with hamburger fat on it. I know from experience.

"Looks like our friend was a little angry last night. Look." Auntie Heather rings the bell again. The waves swirl around the bubble of the world. I already saw that. Except…I take a closer look. It looks like many things hit the bubble and left dents.

"Wow, what did that?" Karly drops her leash and walks closer to the bubble. "Auntie Heather, please ring it again." She puts out her hands and waves them a little. "The Hodag was angry he couldn't get into his hole. Wow. It feels like he tried to paint the ward black. He really is a firebreathing dragon." My Girlpup's eyes are as big as pork chops.

"I think angry is an understatement. While I suspect the only way to see our friend is to come out at night, I don't want to come out alone. And no, you can't come." Auntie Heather puts her bell back in her bag and pulls out some salt and herbs. She grabs one more thing: ropes and wood sticks wrapped together.

Auntie Heather hands the jar of crystal salt cubes to Karly. "Toss a few of these at the ward to break it. Not too much, we don't want to poison the soil or kill the plants." She looks down at the burned charcoal all around her. "Or keep the plants from coming back." She sighs and uncoils the rope thing. There are two long ends that she ties to a tree that isn't as damaged as the rest. Auntie Heather pulls the rope thing apart and tosses the other end into the pit.

"Isn't that the rope ladder from the upstairs bedroom?" Karly pulls the ends of the ladder tight against the tree. She likes to pull on leashes. At least when she wants to go somewhere she thinks is important.

"Uh huh. It's the fire escape ladder from the guest room. Now it's the pit-exploring ladder. I'm going to climb down. Tell me if the knot begins to untie, I don't want to fall. If it's safe, I'll let you come down."

"And if it's not?"

"Send George down."

Auntie Heather knows I am a good fighter and can protect her. Except, I am not so good jumping or climbing ladders. I hope she doesn't run into trouble. It would be embarrassing to hurt The Bad Thing by landing and squashing it. I don't smell/taste it, but you never know. There is so much gassulfurdrysnakecatstink that it's hard to tell. It doesn't feel like it's new. I take a little sample. No, Auntie Heather is right, this is a smell/taste from the night. I can taste dew and moonlight in it and that's not too bad. Baking in the sun doesn't improve the smell/taste. I amble over to Karly and blow out my nose on her jeans. She screams at me. Yeah, well, it's not like I carry a tissue behind my ear. I am not about to use my ear to wipe my nose. That's sick.

Auntie Heather slides her arm through the handle of her bag and climbs into the pit. Karly and I hold our breath.

I'm not sure why.

Why would that help if Auntie Heather gets into trouble?

"I have the flashlight shining on the ladder. You can come down, but be very careful, there are a lot of thick roots that the Hodag just broke off and they're as sharp as spears. Your mom would kill me if I return you with even a scratch," Auntie Heather calls out from the pit. Why is she talking with a towel over her mouth?

I poke my head over the hole. How can The Bad Thing stand to smell itself? Packmom complains I smell houndy and chases me for baths. I smell wonderful—it's the bubbly stuff that reeks. She'd have to use a whole bathtub full of bubbly stuff to wash The Bad Thing, and I am not sure if that would work. Maybe her oilyflowerbitter stuff she puts on for special occasions would help.

Gag.

I turn my head, my eyes are tearing and my nose is itchy. This is the only time I can remember that Auntie Heather and Karly have an advantage with their weak senses.

Karly's voice sounds like she has a mouth full of oatmeal as it floats up from the hole. "It looks like a junk shop down here. I thought dragons collected gold. This is just garbage." I hear things clack and clang. "More broken plates, an old picture of a soldier, jars and jugs, and...oh no."

"Karly, don't touch those. I guess we found the rest of the body. I really didn't want to get the police involved in this, but now I guess we'll have to. Not good. Hodags are part of a witch's duty, not the police's. Unfortunately, dead bodies are theirs."

More clinking and some foot scraping.

The smell/taste swirls up like a tornado of bees and stings my nose. "Arooo," I howl. Enough is enough—I'll fight the Hodag Bad Thing.

First I'll need a nose mask.

And food.

Is it dinnertime? Snack time? My tummy grumbles. I look back into the pit and woof.

"Just a few more minutes, George. Some of this is very interesting. I think these candleholders are silver. Is this a pile of copper wire? What an odd collection, other than these shiny potato chip bags, everything is very old. Move away from the edge, George. Good boy."

I wag my tail. Good boy means a treat. Something flies out of the hole and lands with a thud at my paws. It's a shiny metal thing. I pick it up by the edge and parade around with it shaking my head to tease Auntie Heather as her head pokes up from the edge of the hole.

"Silly dog. That's a picture case. I want to see if we can figure out who is in the picture. Karly, what are you up to down there?" Auntie Heather pulls herself up—her bag is stuffed with moldymetalwoodclay smelltasting things.

Karly sounds like she's talking through a towel now. I play keep-away with Auntie Heather. This is fun!

"George, enough. Give."

I drop my head and drop it into her outstretched hand. Peeps have no sense of humor. Life is meant for fun and play.

"And learning. Sometimes play is learning. Right now we need learn for other reasons. Concentrate on the Hodag, George. I don't think it's a murderer, but I have to wonder why it's here and why it's burning the woods."

She did it again. I narrow my spectacular eyes and look into hers. If I am not allowed in my Girlpup's head, she shouldn't be wandering around in mine.

"That only works for partners. I'm your Packleader and until you and Karly work out your differences, I need to know what you're up to. Even then I might need to check in on you." Auntie Heather's voice is friendly and she strokes my ears. She can do anything as long as she never stops.

Sigh.

Mmm.

I roll into her hand.

"That's enough. Karly, are you ready?" She stops rubbing my ears and walks over to my Girlpup, who is struggling with her own bag of stuff that smell/tastes like rootsrotmushroomsbone. *Peep bones*! We definitely don't need any more of those!

"I want to study them. If they're from what I think they might be, I'll put everything back in the hole and tell the police. Karly, do you want me to take this bag and you can take this smaller one." Auntie Heather must've carried in another bag, 'cause she didn't have that one before.

"Woof." I grab the bag from Karly. I am a strong basset hound. I will carry it.

Or drag it.

I am built well, but I'm a little too short to carry a long bag.

"Thanks for trying to help, but I've got it," Karly says dryly. Hmmm. Is she holding back a laugh? Wish she'd let me into her head. Just in case, I raise my lip in a grin. It's not a snarl, but let her figure that out. She takes the bag from me. I tug a little then give it up. At least I try to help.

"Aren't we going to get in trouble for taking this stuff?" Karly slings the bag over her shoulder and catches up with Auntie Heather. She's moving fast to the parking lot. I put it into high gear. I am faster than Peeps. Karly stomps on the end of her leash and grabs the handle. My head flies back and my back feet are suddenly ahead of me.

Fine.

I don't want to lose her, but she could've just asked. I get up and shake everything back into place.

"If these things represent what I think they do, then the police won't need to know anything. We're going to work on a spell to make these treasures talk about their past. Meanwhile, we need to go back to the parking lot. Oh no. I didn't drive did I?" Auntie Heather lowers her face into her hand. "We need to put these things next to the pit and ward it again. Maybe it's good I didn't have the car or I wouldn't have remembered to protect the pit. We'll come back for this…" she points to the bags, "after the demonstration." They pile the stuff from the pit and Karly pulls me to the trail.

I hope the demonstration means food. I need something to clean my mouth from the smell/taste of The Bad Hodag. Once again, I wish I could spit. Instead, I hack a little.

It's not the same.

Chapter Eleven

There are many Peeps in the parking lot. Some are sitting at picnic tables. More are sitting on the kind of chairs that rip when I jump on them. They are all talking at once and the sound hurts my ears, especially since the woods are so quiet. They are too loud to notice. Peeps need lessons on using their senses and their brains. The world would be a better place for all of us. Hmmm, now what is this all about? Are demonstrations picnics? I seem to remember Karly telling me about a cooking demonstration she did for a class. I pull Karly to a picnic table that smell/tastes good. It smell/tastes so good. I lean into my collar, trying to get closer to the food.

"Knock it off George. I mean it, next time I'll put a training collar on you," Karly threatens. Big threat—I can slip out of any collar. I pull closer to the table. Warm smell/tastes float over my face and nose and catch in my ears and folds. I sit pretty at the feet of a nice-looking youngster. They always drop food and their faces collect all sorts of nom noms.

There she goes. A hot dog slides out of the bun and I catch and swallow it before anyone can blink. I lick my lips and wait for the youngster to drop the bun. She wags it around her head and makes weird pup noises. I smell/taste ketchup. Drool collects and drips in a string until I am connected to the ground. Wait for it. Wait... Got it. I snatch the bun before it hits the ground. All done, I pull Karly over to a group of Peeps standing next to a huge yellow and black machine. I can't even climb up to the door to get in. The bucket in the front is big enough for ten of me.

And some doughnuts.

Sniff. Sniff.

Yup, I smell doughnuts.

"Oh, there you are. I thought I saw you before. Are either of you hungry?" Auntie Heather's busybody friend charges toward us with plates of wonderful-smelling food. I look at her with big hopeful eyes. She can't resist and hands me a half of doughnut. Who am I to argue? I snarf it.

"Belinda. How lovely that you made it. The turnout is fantastic, it's a good thing you brought the food. Oh, and please don't feed George anything, he's on a diet." Auntie Heather sounds fake-happy. I think she's more upset about my snack than she lets on.

Or maybe it's all the food.

Though why a Peep wouldn't want a spread like this at a demonstration is beyond me. I am thirsty. There is a big jug thing dripping something. I lick the thing that sticks out.

"George." Karly makes a disgusted noise. I pant in her general direction. "Just a second." She gets me a plastic bowl of water. It tastes like bad chemicals, but I drink it and shake the rest off my face. My tags come free of the pouch they are kept in and jingle. It drowns out the babble of Peeps talking for no reason. Blah blah blah.

Waste of air space if you ask me.

"We have the signs all ready for everyone." Auntie Heather's busybody friend holds up a board on a stick as she reads it. "The Park Is For All The People, Not Just The Ones That Can Afford It."

I don't get it. The land isn't anyone's, we live on it until we're gone and our puppies take over. Are the big machines going to take the land away? I look for trucks that can take away the earth. My ears almost stand on end when I see that there are some driving in. They are going to take the land away. They can't do that. This is everyone's land!

"Grrr. Aroo!" We can't let them steal the earth. I pull Karly to the line of big trucks.

A huge Peep is standing next to a big black car. He is shouting through a big, empty ice cream cone tilted on its side.

"This area is posted with no trespassing signs. Please leave the area or we'll have to contact the police and have you chaperoned out of this portion of the park. Ladies, we don't own the entire park. Go use the part preserved for recreation." He doesn't sound happy we're here. But if Auntie Heather, Karly, and I don't find The Bad Hodag he will really be unhappy.

Another Peep holds up a sign and shouts, "I don't see any no-trespassing signs. Why don't you go back from where you came from and find a different site to build on? This has been ours for generations. You have no right to it," she says.

The air smell/tastes bitter with fearangerhormones and a touch of peanut butter sandwich.

Ah.

There's a bit of dropped sandwich near my paws.

I scarf it down.

"According to the deed, we have every right to this parcel of land. It was never part of the park. Randolph Singer only allowed it to be used since he couldn't farm it. Too many rocks and hills. By developing this parcel, we will bring money into the community and offer much needed housing to this beautiful town. So, please clear the area so we can do our jobs."

The Guypeep puts down the cone and steps to a large machine. Its wheels are wrapped with metal in the shape of an upside down caterpillar biting its butt. A large square box is on the front. He turns it on and it burps out black smoke. I blow out through my nose. No way do I want to breathe that stuff in. The Guypeep puts the box down to the ground and it sounds like the Earthmom is screaming as it scrapes dirt and grass away from her skin. "Arooooooo!" I bay in sympathy.

This is wrong.

My friends run to the front of the machine, I lead Karly to the front. The Guypeep just slows down.

"People, I know you are all peaceful, concerned citizens, but everything here is legal. You have to leave." The Guypeep shouts over the noisy machine. He pulls a phone out from a pocket and swipes his finger over it. I admit fingers would be nice to have. "Yes Ma'am. Yes. Please do." He swipes the phone again and turns to us. "The police are coming. If you don't want to spend time downtown, I suggest you find your way back to the public park."

More Peeps shout over each other. It sounds like a thunderstorm, rain hitting the roof and thunder crashing. It makes no sense to me. My ears lift a little when I hear a car. It's long, I can tell by the thumps the front and back wheels make as they go over a road bump. It finally drives up and pulls next to the Guypeep. A door swings with a metal swish and a Ladypeep gets out. She smell/tastes of gasoline, fake flowers, and coffee, and something else. Cat? It's a cat. Catcatcat I howl. I am sure I can see cat hair float around her.

I want that cat.

They eat my birds.

They hiss.

They have sneaky claws and paws.

They don't like me.

And I don't like them.

I slip my head out of the collar and amble over to the Catpeep. She doesn't have legs. This is weird—I need to investigate. The cat might be under what she is wearing.

Padding quietly, I come from behind her and slip under what she's wearing. It's dark and smells like soap, sweat, and Ladypeep.

Not cat.

Ah-choo!

"Eeek! What the…!" She lifts her clothes and kicks me away from her. It isn't a hard kick, but still. Why would she do that? I smell cat and only want to see it.

Really.

I wouldn't chase it. Where is it? Peeps don't wear cats as a rule. Maybe her cat sits on her lap.

I run back to Karly. She looks down at me, laughs, and covers her mouth with a hand before she slides the collar back over my head. Everyone around us is laughing. What did the Catpeep do? I look at where she is standing, but I don't see anything worth a laugh. I make a crease in my forehead as my eyebrows draw together. I've seen it in my water dish, and it's very attractive. Peeps laugh at the strangest things. Maybe the cat escaped when I wasn't looking.

The Catpeep's face is growing dark and I seefeel heat surround her. Is she angry at her cat? She starts to sneeze and reaches into her car. She has a wad of tissues and sneezes into them.

"It's illegal to have a dog without a leash, even in the park. When the police come I will make certain you are fined for such blatant disregard of the rules." The Catpeep sneezes some more.

Karly nudges Auntie Heather. "She's allergic to dogs, isn't she? George why did you slip the leash? Now we're in big trouble. Even if it was funny." Karly laughs some more—high-pitched giggles. Auntie Heather puts a hand over her mouth. She can't hide she's laughing too. I don't understand Peeps sometimes.

The Catpeep walks to the Guypeep. "What have you been doing? Why aren't these people gone? The rest of your crew is going to be here in a few minutes and they won't be able to do anything with them in the way."

Auntie Heather speaks up, "That's the point, isn't it? This land was never supposed to be sold, it was granted to us before the town was incorporated. Robert Singer only had custody of it because the deed was in his wife's name. When Rob passed on, we understood the land would be added to the park. None of us understand how your company gained access to it. Until we do, we aren't going to let you destroy a single tree here. This is a sacred place, needed by all, not just by those that will buy a condo from you."

The Peeps around us clap loudly. I'd clap too, but it's beneath me.

I "aroo" instead. Even though I am not exactly sure what Auntie Heather said, it sounds good. Her friends think so, they're still clapping and talking over the Catpeep whose pet ran away. I hear the baying of Badge Dude's car and smell/taste fearsweatanger from the crowd. They look at one another, but no one leaves. The Catpeep and the Guypeep cross their arms over their chests and make hard eyes at us. They aren't very happy. Well, we aren't either. I growl under my breath. They want to own the Earth and that's wrong.

They didn't even pee-mail anyone about it. Not even the Bad Hodag. Hodag! The fur on the back of my neck sticks up. I growl again. It isn't safe, even for the Catpeep and the Guypeep.

Karly snaps her leash, pulling my neck back. "Stop growling, you've gotten us into enough trouble."

I look at her and send pictures of the Hodag through our mental link. The door is locked tight. She doesn't want to know what I am thinking. I whimper and paw Auntie Heather. She looks between my Girlpup and me and sighs.

"Karly, you need to pay attention to George. He's growling because of the Hodag. He's concerned about everyone here. We don't know that the creature is sleeping by day and it could be dangerous. Let's get this resolved and get the stuff back at the Hodag's hoard."

The car drives to the front of the crowd and stops next to the Catpeep's car. The Badge Dude gets out.

I inhale.

It smell/tastes like the same one that came to Auntie Heather's house that one time. Auntie Heather blows out a breath. Why did she hold her breath? She isn't under water and the smell is about the same as before. Silly Auntie Heather. I snort. She turns her head and stares me down. I look at my paws.

The door to the car slams shut and I hear jingling, smell/taste gun/leather/cotton/sweat, and smell/feel heat on my whiskers. I lift my head. The Badge Dude is talking to the Catpeep. I can't hear anything and pull on Karly's leash to get closer.

She stands still.

I pull again.

Karly is a rock I can't roll.

I tilt my head back. She glares at me. Maybe he'll come here and massage my ears.

Woot!

He is coming over. The Badge Dude smiles at us. I smile back and swing my tail in a circle. Hellohellohello friend! I sit and offer my paw and cock my head. I am a very good boy.

Yup.

Pet me.

Feed me.

My tail is spinning, letting them know I need their attention.

"How did George end up off-leash and under Ms. Lanta's skirt?" The Badge Dude asks through a smile. He crouches and scratches behind my ears. He remembers not to pat.

Good Badge Dude.

I praise him with a lick.

My Girlpup answers while tugging on her leash. "He thought he saw something and pulled out of his collar. I'm sorry, it won't happen again. I don't think." She gives me the stink eye. "Will it?"

I fart.

Loudly.

A wonderful, long trumpet call.

"George, are you trying to get us into more trouble?" Karly yells the first part, and then looks over at the Badge Dude and tones it down a notch.

Good.

I duck my head under Badge Dude's hand for more scritches. A little farther over there, please.

Sigh.

He's very good at this.

He speaks in a low tone. I don't think he wants to be overheard. Secrets? Cool! What's the secret? I listen.

"I just found out you're in charge of this fiasco. Can you please ask your friends to go somewhere else? I don't want to have to do the paperwork it would take to bring all of you in. And don't let George escape again—I won't have any choice but to fine you or take him to the animal shelter."

"We aren't doing anything wrong, just a peaceful demonstration—"

The Guypeep interrupts Auntie Heather. "On private property. Ms. Lanta is richer than pudding, but not nearly as sweet. Go over to the park, call the papers, do whatever you want. Just leave this area. Please?"

Auntie Heather looks around at all her friends and frowns. "I'll try, but I'm not making any promises." She brightens and turns her attention to the Badge Dude "Did you find out anything about the bones?"

"The case is as cold as the bones were. We probably won't discover anything about them. Since they were sent in for carbon dating, there isn't going to be anything in our files. Maybe they were from an old pioneer burial. It's not a police matter, whatever they discover now. Unfortunately, your trespassing is."

Auntie Heather looks at all the Peeps surrounding us. They are looking back, waiting for something from her. "May I borrow your megaphone? I don't think I can speak over all these people."

The Badge Dude hands her a cone-shaped thing that smell/tastes like plasticbatterychemicalswires. Auntie Heather flips a switch and clears her throat. There is a terrible shriek. "Aroooo!" I howl in pain. What is that thing doing to her voice?

The Badge Dude takes the thing from her and adjusts something. He hands it back to her. He's smiling. His heart is beating fast and his breath is faster too.

This is interesting.

Auntie Heather holds up the thing and speaks into it. "I'm sorry everyone, we need to move our demonstration to the park proper. There are other ways we can handle this, and believe me," she turns so she faces the Catpeep without a cat, "we will do everything in our power to make sure this land remains available for the use of everyone."

The crowd cheers. Picnic baskets are packed, chairs folded, and garbage picked up. They leave, with nothing to show there were a lot of Peeps here. I hear them in the woods, going to the main part of the park. I tug on Karly's leash, rolling my eyes to white, they are going where the Hodag is. It's dangerous for them. Itisisis!

I must go and protect them. Stupid Peeps! It smells so bad, why can't they smell the badness?

Peeps moan and blahblahblah fills the air. That answers why they don't notice the woods are quiet—they can't hear over their own blahblahblah. I don't even know what they're saying. I ignore them and drag my Girlpup to the edge of the woods. She isn't even arguing.

"Auntie Heather," she says softly. Auntie Heather is talking to The Guypeep and the Badge Dude and Karly isn't supposed to interrupt. Our Auntie doesn't answer. "Auntie Heather?" she says louder.

Auntie Heather turns and puts a finger over her lips.

Uh oh.

Karly is in trouble now. She pulls me back to our Auntie.

Auntie Heather looks down at us and sighs. "Excuse me for a moment." She glares at my Girlpup. Does Auntie Heather have a link to us or not? Right now I wouldn't bet on it. "Karly, what is so important? I need to organize this group." She gestures to the crowd. "I'll be with you in a few minutes."

"Sorry. It's just that George needs to go. Now!"

I am one brilliant basset and quick to understand. I do my potty dance. Jiggle jiggle my rear, stomp stomp, shake my front, cross my legs, and paw at Karly's pants.

Auntie Heather slowly shakes her head and grins. I can tell she thinks I am funny. "Go ahead, then." She returns her attention back to the Peeps after shooing us away.

Chapter Twelve

I yank Karly back to the woods, past the burned and scratched wood that the other Peeps ignore. They don't look down. They don't look up, either. No wonder their senses don't work, they don't exercise them. With their weak senses they need to work out, definite design flaw. We don't have any problems so we share our great abilities. It's a fair trade, since they make our food.

My tummy alarm goes off. Karly hears it, even through her loud pants. Except for the muffled blahblahblahs of the Peeps in the parking lot, we make the only sounds in the woods.

Or, Karly does.

I am a silent hunter on soft paws. The quiet is a creepy feeling. My tummy alarm shuts off and the fur on my ruff rises.

"That's funny—once your stomach starts to rumble it doesn't stop until you eat something."

I stop pulling to smellfeel, smell/taste, and smellhear, but not in that order. Karly bends down and strokes my hackles smooth.

"What's wrong? You're scaring me a little."

I am a brave basset—I am designed that way—but I am worried for my Girlpup. My senses feel dead. There is nothing here.

Nada.

A big zero.

Even my smell/taste is dull. No temperature. Not hot, not cold, not in between. So weird. Magic. Oh, great. The Bad Hodag has magic. Is it here? Now? I flare my nose and open my mouth. I try to cough out the cotton that covers everything. I didn't like it as a puppy in the toys I killed—I don't like it now.

Auntie Heather is gone! Where is she? "Aroo!" Is she gone forever?

Karly continues to pet me and threads from her mind reach mine. She picks up what I am feeling. Nothing but dry cotton in my mouth. I am thirsty. Not hungry. Oh no, I am dead. I know it.

"Don't be silly. Auntie Heather is coming and she'll figure this out." My Girlpup looks into the trees and down at the ground before looking around her. Good Girlpup! She is totally trainable. I am a teacher!

Karly snorts.

I snort back and paw her. What is she seeing? I crane around, but everything is foggy. The silver leashes are still clipped together.

"Not a thing. The sun is out—there shouldn't be fog. AUNTIE HEATHER!"

Her shout hurts my ears. "Barkaroo!" I scold her. She yells again. I claw her leg—one good pain deserves another.

"Stop it. How is Auntie Heather going to find us?"

Actually, that's a good question. Um. Yeah, and how come I can hear Karly when everything else is dead?

"Karly? George? I can feel you're out here. Can you hear me? Come on kids, let me know where you are," Auntie Heather calls out to us. I can just about smell/taste where she is, although her voice is all around us. "Roque found me, but his nose isn't as good as George's and he's having trouble finding you."

"Auntie Heather, we're here!" Karly shouts. Her voice sounds like it's coming from all directions, too.

I smell/taste her. HerbplantcinnamonSnickerdoodle. She's close. "Aroo!" I pull Karly to the sweet smell/taste. Theretherethere! I bounce in place as she comes through the fogcloud.

"Oh thank goodness, I wasn't sure if I'd be able to find you. It appears our Hodag can cast camouflage spells. Who knew? This is going to complicate matters. I set a marking spell behind me. All my stuff is still in my bags, so we'll go back, get those, set up a barrier spell, and go home. Before we come back here I want to find a counter spell for this." Auntie Heather waves her hand around to include the fogcloud. "This is a dangerous trap if anyone comes out here. They'll never get out. I'm not sure if we can find the edges to put up a barrier spell."

We walk, following a shiny ribbon of energy that Auntie Heather gathered and spun through the fogcloud. It isn't long before we are back into the sun. I sniff the edge and lift my leg. I can find the edges.

No problem.

I look up at Auntie Heather. "Ruff. Woo Woo!" I inform her.

"Sounds good, George. Stay here and keep everyone out until we can put up our magical fence," Auntie Heather tells me as she bends down to scritch my back above my tail.

Ohhh. That is the best spot of all. I wriggle into the scritch until she stops. My ears droop. Sad.

Scritches always end too fast.

"Not enough time now. How about a treat when we get back to the house?"

My ears rise and so does my head. I wag. That sounds good.

Even if it will take forever before we finish here.

Auntie Heather clucks and shakes her head as she stands up. "Not forever. Now if anyone wanders over here, keep them away. Karly, come help me with the bags."

My small Pack leaves me. I put my nose to the ground and patrol the edge of the fogcloud. It's easy to find the edge. If I get too close it feels like I am trapped in towels. Not the nice towels that are rubbed over me after a yucky bath.

Suffocating towels trying to stop everything from being.

Towels of death.

I square my shoulders and move with determination, staying away from the fogcloud place. My tail is pointing up with a gentle curve. I lift my head and aroo to the sky. Bad Hodag, I will find and deal with you.

Whatever you are.

The woods smell/taste of burnedsmokemaplesyrup.

I look up.

More scorched trees. The Bad Hodag is killing our woods. I stomple the ground.

Auntie Heather is trying to catch her breath when she reaches me. "What's wrong George? Is the Hodag here? Did you have to scare someone away?" She sets down the bags and wipes her forehead with the back of her hand.

I jump up to one of the burned trees and lean with front paws against the trunk, standing on a root. I woof and crane my neck to look behind me.

"I noticed that earlier. What is going through that animal's mind? It's senseless destruction and that's usually something more typical of my kind."

I am pretty sure she means Peeps. Not witches. They fix things.

"The faster we find it, the faster we can move on to other things. We won't have to worry about the trees burning down if the bulldozers take them down first. I've never felt the woods so disrupted. Have you seen any animals at all?"

Glad one of my Pack finally notices that little fact. Karly plods up to us. I drop down at her feet and offer my belly for a scritch. She's been gone too long. Plus, she didn't take her leash with her.

I don't need it.

"I am sure these are getting heavier, Auntie Heather. The Hodag has magic, maybe it made a gravity spell to make things weigh more if they are carried away from the hoard," Karly complains.

Auntie Heather snorts at my young Girlpup. I do, too. There is no magic tickling my skin coming from the bags. Karly is lazy. They say I am getting pudgy? I snort again, roll over, and get to my paws. She didn't even notice my invitation.

"Did you notice any animal sounds while you were walking?" Auntie Heather takes a bag from Karly and gives her a smaller one.

"No." Karly cocks her head and spins slowly in place. "Where is everything? How come we didn't notice before?"

I look at her with my mouth wide open. Duh, like maybe you were talking, or thinking too loud? Or the herd of Peeps in the parking lot blahblahblah'd everything out of your head? I told you before and I'll tell you again, you need to use all your senses. And learn to use mine. When gifts were passed out, I was number one in line. Yep, Karly needs to use her link with me. She won't learn anything if she won't. I circle the fogcloud, brushing my whiskers to smellfeel the edge.

"Where are you going?" my brilliant Girlpup asks.

I fart as my answer.

Oopsy.

Maybe I need different food? Or at least more. I look behind and give her a soft woof to speed her up. We need to seal the barrier before I starve to death.

"You might want to wait until I prepare the spell. Unless you're just looking for the Hodag, in which case, be my guest. How were you planning on catching it?" Auntie Heather asks the question of the day.

Huh. Never even thought of that.

I know what it smell/tastes like, but I am not even sure how big it is or what it looks like. Book pictures aren't very good for knowing something like that. They're kind of blurry. So are bookwords. Books aren't real. Books are a bad way to store stuff that should be kept in brains. They are only good for chewing on. You don't see familiars, the smartest of all creatures, keep books. No, we know what's important from the very beginning.

Even if we don't *know that* we know it.

Except, I don't know much about the Hodag. Which means only one thing: it's not important.

Auntie Heather reaches into the bag filled with all her stuff—not the Hodag stuff—and pulls out her bell, herbs, crystals, and oils. No candles.

"We don't need them—there's enough energy in the woods and water that we don't have to ask the fire to share its power."

How does she *do* that? Karly looks at me and smiles.

She knows. Somehow she knows Auntie Heather can hear me. Maybe Auntie Heather hears her, too. That would be fair.

"Karly, take these crystals. Put the clear quartz north, the smoky quartz south, the onyx west, and the amethyst east. Hold all the stones in your right hand, but place the crystals with your left. Before you put them down, hold them tight and tell them exactly what you want them to do. I've already moon-charged them, so they're good to go. Why don't you take off the leash, too. George won't need it for this, it'll just get in the way."

Karly looked at Auntie Heather, her lips were puckered, a silly thing Peeps do, and her eyebrows were so close together they almost looked like there was just one. "Um, what am I supposed to tell them? Isn't there a prepared spell or something?" she says as she unclasps the leash from my collar. She clips the end to the hand-loop and puts it around her neck.

Pretty necklace.

"First, not a lot of anti-Hodag spells. Second, just tell them to keep people from wandering into the fogcloud. It's different than hiding a hole. I am not sure we can hide the fogcloud without breaking the magic the Hodag used. Until we get home and can find some reference to null magic, we're just going to ask the crystals to amplify your wish to protect everyone from this trap. At least, I believe this is a trap. It's too obvious to hide anything. I'll meet you here coming from the other direction."

My Girlpup shook her head, without the drool splatter.

Poor Girlpup.

"George, you keep your puh...Karly, from wandering into the fogcloud. I'll follow the path you made. If I run into a problem I'll ring the bell. Or send Roque," Auntie Heather says before she murmurs in a voice that I can barely hear and Karly can't. "I'm spending too much thinking like you."

I roll my eyes at that. She needs to stay out of my mind, period. My Girlpup is the only one that should share it. Roque chatters at me. It sounds like he's laughing.

He is.

Karly and I move away from Auntie Heather. I nudge her left hand and rub my muzzle against the rocks. They smellfeel warm against my whiskers. At each compass point, I mark the spot by lifting my leg. Take that, Bad Hodag—this land is mine! Karly makes gagging noises, but does what she's supposed to do with the rocks. I lick Karly's hand to praise her.

I can't smell/taste/feel or hear Auntie Heather. That should be good, if she rings the bell she's in trouble. She's not in trouble. Unless she's in the magic fogcloud and it killed the sound. Worrying, I pull Karly back to the start. Except...I smell/taste something. It's good.

What is it? Squirrel?

No. Rabbit? No?

It's gamegamegame.

I take off toward the delicious scent and stick my nose in a spot where a bunch of trees grow together.

EEEEEEEEEeeeeeeeeeeeeeeeeeeeeeeeeeeeee!

Fire! Fire is burning my muzzle! Make it stop! Nownownow! Karly! Auntie Heather! Help me! I think I found the Hodag.

Chapter Thirteen

"Why'd you stick your face into a porcupine?" My beloved Girlpup holds onto my cheeks, tipping my head one way, and then the other. She touches a sharp needle and tries to twist it out. "Nooarooooo!" I wail.

"Dogs. They never think beyond the moment." Auntie Heather sprinkles a little oil and drops some leafy bits on the ground I can't smell to finish the circle. She picks up her bag as she walks to us. "Didn't we pull quills from your nose last year? I'll get them out, and then we have to go back to the house to find a better concealing spell. Odd though, I thought all the animals were gone. Karly, did you see the porcupine?"

Karly shakes her head. Her hand moves too and it's still on the sharp needle. I wail again. It was The Horrible Hodag! It has quills! I know it. I smellfeel it.

"WooOOoooo!"

"Guess this is as good a time for another healing magic lesson. Karly, do you remember what to do?"

I think Karly nods because she still has her hand on the needle and the pain burns. It could have been The Horrible Hodag. The smell of it is everywhere.

"It's different than what you learned before. I think George is a bit distracted by his own pain, so you'll have to find the link between you two to share your energy. It's going to sting a bit for both of you. Do you think you can handle it while I pull the quills?"

I hear Auntie Heather shuffle things in her bag. Hurry already!

"My Leatherman. Best tool I ever bought."

Now I hear clicking and metal sounds. The quills burn. I am sure there is blood running down the white of my bib. I whine, and then whimper for good measure. There must be a gazillion burning needles in my poor nose. What is Karly waiting for? I paw her leg. I think it's her leg. I don't care what it is. Hurry and fix me!

Karly's silver mindleash to me is solid and she follows it like a champ. Even though it hurts, I am proud of my Girlpup. Good Girlpup. She finds the red-hot pain spots and draws some through our bond. A shudder runs through the hand that's petting my back.

"Ouch! It didn't hurt like this when we healed the squirrel." Karly stops petting me and the pain builds again.

"You only need to share energy, not take all his pain. Picture white light pouring down that bond of yours. It won't hurt as long if you buffer the pain with healing energy. Just hold the link and let George know you're here for him. If you take too much pain you will be worthless trying to heal him if you're alone. With other creatures, you'll only feel enough so you can recognize the symptoms. George is a part of you, so you'll feel what he feels. Just as you can share his senses. The trick is to balance his pain with your gift of energy."

If I could snort right now, I would. Like Karly is willing to use my amazing senses. Karly slides energy down the leash. The sting goes from the burn I got sticking my tongue on a cold metal pole to warm bathtub water.

OUCH!

"Sorry, George, there are only a few quills. I'll pull them out as quickly as I can."

More hurting. Karly strokes my back.

It doesn't really hurt. It doesn't really hurt. I count rabbits.

One.

Three.

Five.

Two. It hurts. "Aroooowww!"

"All done. Karly, put this ointment on to keep his nose from getting infected. You did just fine. It's a little easier with our patients. We don't have that link to fall into their pain. It's a little harder because we don't know exactly where it hurts. Everything is balance and a trade-off."

Clicking.

I try to see what Auntie Heather is doing, but my nose is swollen and I am afraid to move it. Karly rubs behind my ears. I put my head between my paws and sigh.

"Look at these quills." Auntie Heather must be talking to Karly, I am not looking at anything. "They aren't banded with the right colors. There aren't green and orange porcupine's."

"Let me see," my Girlpup says.

My nose feels a lot better, so I open my eyes to see the weird quills. I am not sure what green and orange mean, Peeps have too many colors to name, but they aren't the white-banded black like a normal porcupine. I get a little closer when Auntie Heather holds them lower for me.

I sniff very gently. No way do I want those things in my nose again. They smell like The Horrible Hodag. It was hiding in its nest and I found him. Er, her. Whatever. I found it. If I can find it once, I'll find it again. Now. I put my nose to the ground and head for a clump of trees. Not the right trees.

"George! Come back here. You need your leash and you can't go after that thing alone. George! Come!" Karly shouts like I'm the pup here, not her. And what's with the "my leash" thing? I grumble at her and stomp my paws to put her back in her place.

She might be right, though. I am not sure I could take down The Horrible Hodag right now. My nose isn't swollen anymore, but it still burns a little. I amble back to my Girlpup and she clips on her leash.

My Peeps pick up the bags. I don't like leaving and my hackles are up. Something is watching us. I hope Auntie Heather can find a way to trap The Horrible Hodag.

Chapter Fourteen

We are at Auntie Heather's house again. I am sleepy, but Auntie and Karly are making a racket tossing around books and it's hard to nap. I try to bury myself under a couch pillow. Roquefort thinks it's funny to push it off. I give him big, beautiful basset eyes to leave me alone. He chitters and throws a cushion at me. I could hate him. Without thumbs like his I can't throw anything back. I am too tired to even lift my lip at him. Healing is hard on a body.

"I must've gone through every book you have, Auntie Heather. There is nothing about Hodags other than the picture you found," Karly whines from the table across from where I am trying to chill. Cupboards are wide open and bookshelves are empty. There are stacks of books everywhere. It looks like a library threw up.

I know why the Girlpup's whiny. We haven't eaten in a week and we've been here forever. They've ignored my reminders. I did my best trick, playing dead, and it didn't work. Roquefort offered me some of his fish. There was only enough to make me hungrier. My tummy growls remembering how it was teased so evilly. I am going to starve to death. I look at my side. Just as I thought, my ribs are showing. I moan.

There is a funny smell/taste in Auntie Heather's house. It's different from Auntie's normal herbplantcinnamonSnickerdoodle patience. It takes a lot of patience to work with Karly. I know firsthand, and basset hounds are experts at patience. It's just how we roll. At first I think it's anger.

No. I don't smell/taste hotsharppepper anger. This smell/tastes more like Karly's normal frustration. It overpowers both Karly's and Auntie Heather's smell/taste—bittersaltysouryellow. Worse, no one is talking.

This worries me. I am a superbasset, but I can't make The Horrible Hodag go away alone. I find game for the Pack. The Pack brings it down and cooks it.

We eat it.

Perfect partnership. While I am a perfect hunting machine, it also means I know my limits. No good to anyone if you trip over your ears trying to get your prey. Not that any self-respecting basset would trip over his ears. Or retrieve them by accident. Well, maybe as a pup.

Only once. Or twice.

I ooze off of the couch with grace and smell/taste the books. Now I know I can find The Horrible Hodag they need to do their part and catch it. Safely. Those needles hurt. I am lucky it didn't bite me and steal my bones. My hackles rise and I growl a little at the thought. It isn't as little as I think—it's louder than my tummy's grumbles.

Auntie Heather pulls down another book from a very high shelf, about her chest height. This one smell/tastes of saltydryteachewymusty old leather and paper. The cover is dark and so are the pages. There is a lot of squiggly writing, and pictures.

Nothing good to eat stuck on the pages, so it's not a cookbook. Must not be any spells against Horrible Hodags since she slams it shut and puts it on a tall pile of books they've already looked at. It shakes and tumbles to the ground.

Auntie Heather says a word that is also used for what they clean up when I go potty, and starts to stack the pile back up.

I inhale all the smell/tastes, roll them over my tongue and slide them over the roof of my mouth. There is magic in all the books, but only one also smell/tastes like The Horrible Hodag.

I am drawn to the pile that Auntie Heather is working on. Drool drips from my mouth to clean my taste buds from the awful smell/taste. Skunk is much better. I nose the rotten book, knocking the pile over again.

"George, why did you do that?" Auntie Heather and Karly both say at the same time. They look at each other and giggle. My Pack is getting loony.

'Kay, now the book is under all the other ones. I paw the pile and use my snout to push it free. I am about to grab it with my mouth when Auntie Heather reaches down and snares it.

"Do you want to explain why this book has your interest?" Auntie Heather riffles through the pages. "Interesting, it's the same one we looked at earlier. The one with the Hodag picture." She bends down to me and gives me a puzzled look. "There isn't anything else in here."

I woof and paw her knee. Figure it out Auntie Heather, put the book down so I can show you. I know you're in my mind. I raise my eyebrows to push the idea of taking another look.

I smellfeel the magic prickle my whiskers. Even an ancient witch with tons of experience like Auntie can make mistakes. From her appearance, she really doesn't have a clue. Auntie Heather's eyes widen and she smiles. Roque trots to her and climbs up to her shoulder. It's really a nifty trick. Wish I could do it, but bassets are built for better things. Not for climbing our Peeps. Still, it's a nifty trick.

Roque sniffs the book and sneezes. I don't know if he tastes anything unless he washes it first. He chitters at Auntie Heather. She opens the book to the Hodag page and puts it in front of me. Well, finally. She must be tired. She took a long time to figure what I want. Is that why she hasn't fed me anything yet?

She brushes hair out of eyes that have big swollen bags under them. If they were droopier they'd look quite wonderful. "George, concentrate now. Keep your mind on the subject, which is the Hodag and this book. Can you do that?" She's cranky as a snapping turtle. Why blame me? There wouldn't be a problem if she didn't have to rely on the stupid books.

I shake myself and nose the page. The magic is very prickly and I pull my nose up. It's like I am dragging my paws on the carpet and getting stung by spark flies. They like coming out when the heat is on during the win...

"George! Concentrate. You sense something and I am too tired to keep up with your thoughts," Auntie Heather growls. Yeesh. Wow, she's good. It's no fair. She can growl *and* get into my mind. I'm not allowed to growl and I can't get into her mind.

Not that I'd want to.

I concentrate on surrounding my nose in white light. A simple spell to protect my nose by using the energy that is stabbing my nose to turn it inside out. I hope I can still smell/taste through it. I can if I am going through pricker bushes, but this is magic, who knows?

My nose is glowing white as I touch the page. It's thicker than the rest, magic holding other pages together like there's honey sticking them together. I drool at the thought.

A wet blob hits the page and the magic smell/feels hotshinymusky. The pages flap apart like Herb the crow coming in for a landing and settling his feathers. Kind of black like him, too. Hah, proof my basset drool is magical.

I didn't know that was going to happen. It did, though. I put my nose between the pages and draw it back. It smell/tastes like The Horrible Hodag. Auntie Heather lifts an eyebrow.

With a hint of chocolate frosting.

Hmmm. The frosting isn't on the pages. I look up to see Karly unwrapping a cupcake. That isn't fair. "Aroo!" I yell at her to share.

Karly dips down and hands me a liver brownie. She almost hits heads with Auntie Heather who is bent picking up the book. I sit back and enjoy my brownie. Roque chatters and uses his fingers to point to his mouth. Karly tosses him a piece of tuna fudge.

"That isn't very smart, Karly. Now George is going to want a piece of the tuna fudge and Roque will want the brownie." Roque points to his mouth and I sit up and drool. "I told you," she says, sighing.

"It's Sunday, isn't it? You won't be able to stay tonight. Go on home and have dinner. If you get a chance see what else you can find on our Hodag. I'll see what I can find on these pages George found and tell you tomorrow, all right?"

Karly groans. "That's totally unfair. We've worked so hard to find clues and now I have to go home?"

I am waiting for my Girlpup to stomp her foot, like The Creep does. She's crabby. Silly Girlpup, if we eat something we'll all feel better.

I nudge her and roll over, playing dead. My tummy is gurgling, starving.
Food.
Now.

Or at least a bowl of liver brownies. That would be very good. I drool again. Snacks are good. They just aren't enough. "Gurgle." I look at Karly with big eyes.

"Do you pro...mise," Karly stretches the word out as long as a dachshund, "to wait until tomorrow before you do anything?" Karly needs to learn trust skills. Auntie Heather can't do anything without me. Roque is good, but he's no basset hound.

"It's going to take a while to figure out what these pages George found mean. Besides, Roque and I need you, the more energy we raise, the stronger we are. Magic is usually a team sport. Haven't I taught you that?"

Karly nods.

Auntie Heather rummages around a cabinet and pulls out a bag of Snickerdoodles. I can smell/taste them. Sweetsugarygoodness. She gives the bag to Karly. Why doesn't she give me a bag? I am starving to death here.

"There's enough to share with everyone." Auntie Heather gives me a long look. She better mean me too. "Including George and your brother. No snitching any until you have your dinners. Now go on home before your mother gets mad at me for taking up so much of your time. She's barely seen you the last few days. Hopefully the Snickerdoodles will keep me in her good graces."

"No problem. What time will I see you in the morning?" Karly looks in the bag and licks her lips. Peeps do that when something smells nummy. Dogs do that when we want to calm someone down, but we also use it when something smell/tastes nummy. She didn't know they were Snickerdoodles. Peeps have no senses.

"I'll call you. Depending on what we need to do, I'll either need to pick you up, or you can ride your bike here. Do you want a ride home?"

Karly shakes her head.

That means no.

"Well go on before your mother shoots me."

Karly snaps her leash on me and we amble home. With a few pee-mail stops on the way.

Chapter Fifteen

"Where's Joey? He said he was going to try to find you and your aunt this morning," Packmom calls out the second we get in the door. That's so wrong. Where is my supper dish is the real question. The Creep can get his own food.

My Girlpup unsnaps her leash. I run over to my corner, tail thumping a tune of impatience against the floor as I sit and wait. Look, I've waited long enough. Feed me. I pant. It's been a hard day. I've worked like a dog.

Heh.

Karly's face is scrunched up in confusion. Not the first time today, poor Girlpup. "He wasn't with us. He isn't supposed to butt, um, bother us when Auntie Heather and I practice my magic. He gets bored and drives us nu... um, he doesn't like it."

Good catch Girlpup, from the look on Packmom's face. Now, let's see. Where is my supper bowl hiding? "Rooooo." I wish I could say food or treats, but basset mouths are made for better things.

Like eating.

My tummy grumbles and growls. Nothing says hungry like a tummy alarm.

Packmom looks at me like she's never seen a basset before and her hands are clenched white-tight.

"Karly, I need to call Heather. Now." She glances at me. "Feed George before he eats the table."

Hey. I don't eat furniture.

Well, as a puppy when my big teeth were coming in, but not since then.

I am not a beaver. They're big fat things with slaphappy tails. Their only goal is to dam up the creek that goes into the big river in the park. My goal is to scare them off. They don't have any respect for my authority. Roque's pulled apart their den a few times. They don't belong on our water. Auntie Heather says they have as much right as we do. We don't try to make lakes. They can go back to Beaverland.

I hear the wonderful taptaptapping of kibble falling into my supper dish and then the dull thuds as it fills. The smell/taste of chicken-salt-flour-garlic-chicken fills my mouth and nose. A strand of my magical drool puddles on the floor. The floor doesn't peel away to show any secrets. It does melt some of a dry, muddy pawprint. Wonder when I left that. It's mine—I don't smell/taste anyone else here. Hmmm. My Pack is slacking off on cleaning our den. I spread my drool around with my paw and the puddle turns brown. Basset drool is multipurpose.

Karly plunks my bowl in front of me. No candles or flowers. Sheesh, do they think I am uncivilized? I dive into my bowl, the smell/taste/feel passing through my mouth and nose as I crunch my way through my meal. I grunt a little at the joy of filling my tummy.

My nose hits the bottom of my supper dish.

Hey.

I look around. Where's the rest? Where's my supper? I still smell/taste the goodness, but there must be more. Maybe under the bowl?

I kick the plastic dish into the wall. It bounces off with a loud clack. I sniff the floor where the bowl was. There isn't anything there. I walk over to the bowl. There are other scratches on the wall. They look like the one I just made. Wonder where they came from? I wrinkle my eyebrows and sniff my bowl one more time.

Nothing.

Sigh.

"George, what did you do? Oh ick. You didn't have to paint the floor with your muddy paws. Mom, I can't find any towels."

Packmom is on the phone. She glares at Karly. "It's right in front of your nose, exactly where they've been since you've were born." She turns her attention back to Auntie Heather's voice. I can hear everything with my superbasset ears. It can be a distraction—fortunately it comes with an off switch. If I am busy, I don't need anyone calling my name and distracting me. Unless they have food.

"How long has he been gone, Doreen?"

Packmom looks at the collar on her wrist. "He left after his snack, about ten this morning. Where do you think he went?"

"There was a big gathering at the park today to demonstrate against the development. He may have gone there. Still, he should be back by now. Call Brian and the police. Why don't I grab Karly and George? With his nose, he should be able to find Joey and there'll be one less thing for you to think about."

Packmom eyes are round and she's very white. Her breathing is fast and she smell/feels frantic/adrenaline/sweat. She's very upset that The Creep is missing. I guess I have to find him. I stretch and pull Karly's leash off the door. No use having two lost Pups tonight.

Chapter Sixteen

I hate cars. My nose and mouth burn from the chemicals. It makes my mouth taste like I licked a hot road. At least Karly isn't dragging me. I settle in the back seat, wishing the window was open so I can stick my head out.

"Too dangerous. You could easily get something in your eyes. We'll be there in a minute."

Minutes, like sand in an hourglass, take forever. Or something like that. What's an hourglass? I shake my head free of the alien thought. Hmmm. Auntie Heather is in my mind again. I sigh.

"So what are we going to do? If Joey is in the fog we'll never find him," Karly sounds tired. It's been a long day. Did she eat yet? Not good for young witches to forget to eat.

Food is power.

Auntie Heather taps her fingers on the wheel while we are stopped. Why do we stop in the road sometimes and not other times? "No one can find the fog spot except other witches, and I've called out Belinda and Tamara. Belinda promises not to share anything. If she does I'll seal her mouth shut." The car moves again.

Karly giggles. Auntie Heather gives her a quick glance and Karly swallows. The chain between us is linked and I feel she is still laughing. I wonder if Auntie Heather can seal a mouth shut. Sure would be handy for some dogs that are always barking at me when we pass their houses.

Now it's my turn as Auntie Heather turns her head and looks at me. I wrinkle my face. I wonder if Roque knows how to block her out. Wish I knew how to ask him.

"So what are we going to do?" My Girlpup asks again. Auntie Heather doesn't seem very focused.

"First we're going to search the woods, just in case Joey got lost or hurt. If we can't find him, we'll have to try to break the fog spell and hope the Hodag doesn't have him."

Would that really be bad?

"George!" Auntie Heather growls.

Sheesh.

Aren't dogs allowed to think without getting scolded?

I hate to argue with Auntie Heather, but how do we break the fogcloud spell? If we do find it, what then? Did she find a Horrible Hodag trapping spell in the pages I found?

Karly is bouncing on her seat. She should've gone potty before we left. I shake my head at the foolishness of young pups.

"Settle down. We'll find your brother." Auntie Heather should find a place for Karly to do her business first.

My Girlpup puts her hand on the back of the seat, turns, and shows me angry eyes. "George! I don't need to potty. Geez."

I realize that the leash link is still connected. Now I get that she's bouncing because she's worrying about The Creep.

"His name is Joey. What if he's hurt, or dying, or…" Karly's voice squeaks and trails off. How embarrassing. She is really worrying about her brother, our Packmate. Well, yeah, I worry too. He's Pack and it's my job to protect him. I am a big enough dog to admit I am wrong.

I slide to the floor and put my nose through the crack between the front seats. I nuzzle Karly's arm and lick her skin. It's GirlpupPeepsaltysoap. She skritches my ears and puts her face against mine. Now I smell/taste painsaltwater. I lick away tears and peer into her eyes, letting her see through mine. She's a brave Girlpup who can learn and do what we need to do. I cover my thoughts so she doesn't catch the 'whatever it is we need to do.' I hope Auntie Heather has something figured out.

We're at the park and Auntie Heather pulls into a spot near the woods. There's a car with flashing lights already there and lots of Peeps. How'd they beat us here?

Karly and Auntie Heather get out of the car and Karly opens my door. I bolt through the opening to escape the fast-rolling crate. Hate it, unless I can hang my head outside the window. My Girlpup grabs her leash, snags me by my collar and snaps the lead on. We don't need her to get lost. She'll be safe with me.

I don't smell/taste any other dogs. Hmmm. No birds or animals other than Peeps, either. It's dark and the woods go on forever. There should be something there. I inhale with an open mouth. Where's The Horrible Hodag's trail? I don't smell/taste gassulfurdrysnakecatstink. That isn't good. Is he in the fogcloud?

They should've brought in more sniffer dogs, even if they are inferior to me. Maybe there are more smell/tastes deeper in the woods and more noses make light work. Peeps are useless when it comes to common senses. Well, then it's up to me to find The Creep. I can do it.

I sigh, spin three times for the magic protection spell, and melt into a down next to Karly. The Badge Dude is talking to Packmom, Packdad, and Auntie Heather. Hmmm. Interesting. He's talking to Packmom and Packdad, but looking at Auntie Heather like she's the most interesting thing here. Auntie Heather's looking back at him and she smell/feels of warmcinnamonbutteroranges. He smell/feels of cinnamonapplejuice. It's so sweet I look around to see if there's any food around.

Nope.

It's spring. They just like each other. Peeps don't do the normal thing in spring and check each other's ears and butts to see what the other smell/tastes/feels are.

In my experience, they'll dance around each other like bees around flowers— getting close, moving away, and close again until they figure it out. Peeps have very poor communication skills.

"Mr. and Mrs. Weldeen, we have people checking out the neighborhood for Joey. They're looking for an eight-year-old boy with a shiny, silver colored bike helmet, an orange Harley-Davidson T-shirt, and riding a black bike, right? Anything else that can help us find him?"

Packmom shakes her head as tears roll down her cheeks. If she were lower I'd groom her face clean.

"No, I told you everything. He left at ten this morning and told me he was going to find out what Heather and Karly were doing today in the park. Karly came home without him and there hasn't been any sign of him since this morning." Packmom's voice is weak and wavery.

She needs to trust me.

I won't let her down.

"Anything you can think of Mr. Weldeen?"

"I left for work before Joey and Karly were up this morning. I don't even know what he was wearing." Packdad's hands are at his sides and clenched so tight that if his nails were long they'd puncture his skin.

"I don't want to worry you any more than necessary, but have you noticed anything odd lately? Someone that you may have thought was following you or your family? Anything unusual at all?"

Packmom's eyes are blinking fast and a waterfall of tears spills from her eyes. I smell/taste bitingbitteracid fear from her. From Auntie Heather and Karly, too.

This. Is. Not. Good. There is a Horrible Hodag out there that leaves bones for me to find. I hope Auntie Heather really found a way to make the fogcloud go away. Did she have enough time? Without my nose, mouth, and whiskers I am as useless as a Peep. That's pretty useless. Even with my magic, I need all my senses.

Why would The Horrible Hodag steal The Creep? Karly glares at me. Er, Joey. We've trounced around the woods forever and it didn't bother us. Except for when I stuck my nose into it. It must've recognized my great power as a protector.

Unless…were other Peeps taken by it? Maybe all the animals and birds? Will I need to fight The Horrible Hodag? My sleek perfection is designed for finding prey, not bringing it down. I am a cuddler—not a killer. If I have to, I can kill evil squirrels or stupid plant-eating rabbits. Not sure about monsters with sharp, pokey quills.

This needs magic. The kind that witches and familiars work together. If the witches stored their memories in their brains instead of rotting books, we'd know what to do now. Familiars support Peeps' spells 'cause familiars can't speak the words right. The Earthmom is all about balance and so is magic.

We balance our witches. Otherwise nothing would get done.

Like now.

Peeps don't use that thing in their heads. We have the common senses; they have the words. Even Auntie Heather, as old as she is, still needs more common sense. That's not something that's easily taught no matter if a witch has a lot of familiars during her long life. I sigh thinking about how much a witch has to learn.

Auntie Heather nudges my paw with her toe. "If you're done feeding your ego, we need to go find Joey."

I get up, lean back into a bow on my hind legs, rock forward, straighten and stretch my front legs and stand. A good shake from head to tail and I am good to go.

I am a hunter and ready to catch my quarry. Or at least find it.

Auntie Heather turns her attention to the Badge Dude that likes her. "Officer James, would it be all right if I take Karly, Belinda, and George with me to look for Joey. We all know the woods well and George has certainly proven how talented his nose is."

"I assumed you'd be involved in the search." The Badge Dude pulls out a small bit of paper and touches Auntie Heather's hand as he passes it to her. 'Kay, Peeps, there are better things to worry about, aren't there? Get your minds out of the clouds, please. I hate spring.

"Call that number if you find anything," he says with too much white showing in his smile. Looks almost like a snarl.

"Of course I will," Auntie Heather smiles back. There is a Horrible Hodag out there probably making dinner of The Creep and she is smiling. This is serious business, not smiling time.

"What's your number Ms. Martin?" He has a small pad and a pen out, ready to write. He can't remember a number? This is what Peeps are made for—storing memories. Silly creatures. Auntie Heather takes the stuff from him and scratches something with the pen onto the paper. She hands it back with that stupid smile.

Ick. Springtime. That's got to be it.

Time to find a mate. Now, if a cute basset Girlpup dog moves into the neighborhood, it'd only friendly to stop and say hi. Always willing to do my part to increase the Pack. I wouldn't be all stupid about it.

"George. George? George! Stop daydreaming. We have work to do." Was Auntie Heather blushing? That's why it's good to have a fur coat, can't see me blush. Not that I ever would need to.

Auntie Heather bends down with one of The Creep's dirty T-shirts. As if I don't live with him, and forgot what his smell/taste is. I sneeze concentrated saltmudpondfrogsourboy. Never changes unless he's is eating, or with his friends, and then he smells like a Boypup cocktail, I like his smell/taste best while he's eating. Boypup smell/taste isn't bad in general.

Auntie Heather whispers to me, "It's just to make this look good. You know exactly what to do, you brilliant boy."

She says just the right thing. I am not sure why they want him back, but he is a member of my Pack. I grin, raise my tail, and put my nose to the grindstone, err, ground.

Smelltasting, sniffing, snorting to clear my palate and sniffing again.

I search for his scent, nose high to catch anything in the air, nose low to catch any smell/tastes on the ground trapped in the plants and the dirt.

There! My tail sticks straight up, an exclamation point to tell Auntie Heather and Karly I am on the right track. "Arroooooo!"

I pull on Karly's leash. The smell/taste is old. Easy enough to follow, but if they want him back fast we need to move it.

"Hurryhurryhurry," I bay. On the track! "Hereherehere!" Karly, speed your butt up!

Karly is slowing me down too much. I could stop fast, which would loosen the leash and make it easy to slip my head out of the collar, but then I'll lose her.

Too much trouble to find two pups when I have her already.

I snuffle a sigh and keep pulling.

"George, you're pulling my arm off!" Karly scolds me. It's her brother whose arm is at risk. She picks up my thought and runs faster.

Roquefort's smell/taste stops me for a moment. I look behind me. He's got my rear. That's what friends are for.

The trail swirls all around me. The air is filled with saltmudpondfrogsour smell/taste. I can't tell where it's going. Karly trips when I slow down to get my bearings. She jerks hard on her leash as she falls over something. Peeps are too tall. I grab the leash and pull it out of her hand. Leatherrubberplastic mixed with footsweat with the main note of saltmudpondfrogsour fills my head. I would've found it if she hadn't tripped over it by accident.

My Girlpup tries to take it away from me. I tug it back. "George, give!" She is actually commanding me to do something. I'm very proud of her. In a "gee, maybe she has a spine" way. Though, of course, I don't want her to do it again. Opening my jaw I drop the shoe neatly into her hands.

Salty tears roll down Karly's face. "Oh, no! It's Joey's sneaker. George, find the other one."

I don't smell/taste or see another shoe, even after scuffing the leaves away. Peeps don't usually walk around with only one shoe. At least, I don't think so. Joey is a Boypup, though. Maybe he lost it running. Running from The Horrible Hodag?

Chapter Seventeen

Auntie Heather catches up to us and looks at the sneaker Karly's holding. She takes it, turns it around and around, her face forming those beautiful wrinkles.

"This is Joey's shoe, for sure?" She's got it in one hand and puts her other on Karly's shoulder.

Karly nods, more tears spilling from her eyes. Tears are weird. Dogs don't do tears. Waste of salt and water if you ask me.

Not that anyone ever does.

I paw her leg. Auntie Heather moves her hand and my Girlpup bends down to hug me. I lick the tears off her face. My Girlpup needs me.

Auntie Heather walks around the area. Silly, she can't smell/taste anything, she's a Peep. What's she doing? Roquefort trails behind, scrubbing his nose. Or sniffing his paws. Hard to tell with a raccoon.

"Can you feel it?"

Karly and I shake our heads. I trundle over to Auntie Heather. There's nothing to…there's a dead spot in front of us. No sound, smell/tastes/feels.

Nothing.

Just more fogcloud.

We all run toward the spot—I am fast on my paws—my Pack behind me so I can protect them. Except there's nothing to protect them from.

How does The Horrible Hodag do that?

"It's spreading," Karly says through tears. "What are we going to do now? What if it fills the whole woods?"

I sniff, hoping to find Joey's scent. If I could find where he went in, maybe Karly could get a rope and pull us out when I find him.

Auntie Heather rustles through the bag she carried with her. "I wish I'd had more time with the book at the house. I brought it with the hope maybe we could figure something out quickly. If the ceremony needs special tools, it's going to take time to gather them—and we don't have a lot of time if Joey's in there." She points to the fogcloud. As if we don't know he is.

The book is pulled out with another rustle. It smell/tastes funny here. Like what? Bittersweetsalttears. Not Auntie Heather's. Books don't cry. Oh, yeah, it's magic. I guess it can do anything.

Well, then, so can I. I yank my head back and pull Karly's leash out of her hands. My neck is very strong. I trot to the blankness. My head jerks back as Auntie Heather stomps on the handle. I try to pull away. She lodges a foot in the loop, trapping me.

Neat trick.

"Even if you had a longer line, I wouldn't let you in there. You and Karly already tried that. Finding Joey by wandering around in that fog is worse than trying to find a needle in a haystack."

What's a haystack?

"Concentrate. I'm not sure you could feel him even if you two managed to bump into each other." I stop pulling. I know better. "Stay calm and help me work through these pages. Roquefort, do you feel anything from the book?"

Roque crawls up Auntie like she's a tree and looks over her shoulder. I wish I could do that. I'm glad she's talking to him so I can hear. I hate not knowing what's going on. Auntie Heather must overhear my Girlpup's and my conversations.

Since she seems to be in my head already.

She shakes hair out of her face and takes her foot off my leash.

"Keep out of trouble." Auntie Heather licks a finger. I could help her with that, even if it is a weird thing to do. It isn't grooming time. She flips through the book until she reaches the pages I found. She looks at Roque who is pointing to something on the page.

Handy.

I wish I had fingers. Looking at my gorgeous paws with their strong claws and at Roque's little hands with only sharp nails I change my mind. My nose is good for pointing. I am perfect as I am. A strong, magical familiar with an abundance of gifts.

Pant. Pant. Pant.

Drops of saliva fall from my mouth. Is it getting hot? Karly pulls her shirt away from her neck. Sweat drips from Auntie Heather's nose. Roque is staring in the direction of the river. Probably looking to take a swim in the cool water. Yup, it's good to be me. I pant and sweat from my paws. It makes them smell like popcorn.

Yum.

Popcorn.

Does Auntie Heather have snacks in her bag?

She kneels next to me, Roque sitting on her shoulder, fingers clinging to her neck. Auntie Heather shifts her shoulder. He chatters something and moves his paws to the top of her head.

"So, does anyone see or feel anything from this?" She turns each page from the group I released at the house.

Magic raises a short Mohawk from my neck to the base of my tail. It prickles. Karly is sitting cross-legged across from our auntie. Her forehead is crinkled in concentration, she shivers and goose bumps cover her skin. The magic is strong. Now to figure out where it's coming from.

I place my nose on the open page where I feel the most zappage. The heat is getting stronger. I can't tell if it's coming from the book or the fogcloud. The page is cool. I slide my nose over pictures I don't remember seeing before. My nose is dry from the heat and I give my strong black scenting machine a good lick with my long tongue. I feel better and touch the page again. Roque bends over Auntie Heather's head to see better.

His teeth clatter and he purrs with excitement. He points out a picture of a tree with a clawed-up trunk. A cloud shape covers the top.

I move my muzzle to the tree. As my wet nose touches the picture the air shimmers and letters slowly darken across the page.

Meaningless shapes.

Hopefully Auntie Heather and Karly can read them. I do worry about the Boypup, it's been a long time and The Horrible Hodag has horrible quills. I don't want The Creep to get punctured. It hurts like fire.

I try to think of his good points. He drops nummies sometimes. When he was little I groomed his face. It was always covered with snacks and baby drool.

Yum.

I drool on the page and the words stop darkening.

Karly looks at the page and back at me. "Look, George's snot and drool made the words show up. The picture changed too." My Girlpup points with excitement. I look again. What do you know? The fogcloud lifted from the tree. The air around the book is cool, too. Sweet.

"George saves the day!" My Girlpup cheers. Roque coughs and climbs off his perch and leans into my Girlpup's legs. She continues to stroke him. Auntie Heather must have very strong shoulders, the raccoon isn't a lightweight. "And you too, Roquefort." Karly reaches over my head to scritch behind Roque's ears. Hey, what about me? I did the hard part. I nudge under Karly's other hand to get my own ear rubbies.

"Can you read it?" My Girlpup stops rubbing Roque's and my ears and takes the book, turns it upside down, shakes her head, and gives it back to Auntie Heather. "What's with the cloud in the tree? What's it mean?" She is talking so fast that spit is raining over the page. The letters begin to fade. I quickly nose the page and they darken again. Everyone gives a sigh of relief.

Except me. I am confident in the power of my wet nose.

Auntie Heather stands with the book. She paces back and forth. Back and forth. Back and...whoo, enough already, you're making me sick.

She peers over the top of the book at me. "Hmmm. I think we can do this."

"Do what?" my brilliant Girlpup asks. She's chewing on a fingernail. Silly thing to do—she doesn't let them grow out to do any good digging or scratching.

Auntie Heather taps the page with the eraser end of a pencil. When did she get that? "We need to light fires all around the fogcloud. We'll add the herbs from the concealing spell and conceal the fogcloud." Auntie Heather beams.

"Seriously? We're going to conceal a fogcloud that conceals things?" My Girlpup's eyes have a lost look. Sometimes I worry she'll never understand magic. Yep, Karly's a witch, she can do magic. I'm a familiar, I am magic. Oh, and a magnificent creation. She stills needs to learn that magic isn't found in a cookbook. I twist my head to the book. Well, most magic isn't found in a cookbook.

I'm going to get sparkly stuff up my nose again when they perform the spell. I sneeze with the memory.

"It should work. Whatever is under that fogcloud will show up once it's concealed. Then we'll find Joey." Auntie Heather pulls stuff out of her bag. I sneeze again just for the heck of it. Roquefort wipes his eyes. Guess my sneezes were too close to him. "That's enough, boys. Karly, take them and see if you can't find enough branches to make a ring of fire."

My Girlpup paces around the fogcloud. "How big a ring? This thing is huge."

Good point. All I can see is a wall of the stuff. Not sure where it ends. I follow my nose, trying to get a feel for the border. Auntie Heather stomps on my leash again. Sigh. This is Karly's, not mine. Take it off already.

"Let's just do this part in front of us. If it works, and we need to, we can work our way back." Auntie Heather stoops to pick up some twigs. She grimaces and puts a hand on her back. Healer, heal yourself. I'll get the branches. Those twigs are useless for a good fire anyway.

The bigger twigs are off the deer trail we walked in on. I trot over to a large one. There is a stupid rock in the way and my claw catches on it.

"Arrroooouch!" That doesn't feel good. Guess I do need my nails cut. I limp to the branch, grab it, and carry it to edge of the fogcloud.

Karly drops a load of sticks and bends next to me. "Broke that one across the top. Auntie Heather, can we fix it, he's bleeding a lot."

Auntie Heather lifts her head from the book. "Excuse me? Oh my. We should do something about that and we need to be quick about it. I'm very worried about Joey, and you must be as well."

Karly and I form the bond we made when we healed the furry-tailed rat, Auntie Heather looking on. She wraps a few green leaves around the claw and the heat from Karly's and my bond makes it feel better. I shake it, the leaves fall off, and my nail is much shorter than it was. Well, if we can make it work once…

"Get back to work, Joey's life might be at stake," Auntie Heather snaps. "I'm sorry. I…" She breaks off. Yeah, understandable. Peeps can't do more than one thing at a time.

Karly and I look at each other and grab sticks, twigs, and branches. We drop them into a wall just a little shorter than me. Roque follows behind us, rearranging all the sticks. Perfectionist. I roll my eyes at him. He doesn't notice, too busy putting the twigs in some order only he knows. Auntie Heather sprinkles the herb mix from a pouch onto the wall. I never realized it looked like a sock. When she empties the pouch I amble over and nuzzle it. It's a sock.

I want it.

Auntie Heather bops the empty sock across the top of my nose. "Stop being silly. I added some things to the mixture to prevent anything other than the wood you collected from burning." She pulls out a match and lights the wall. Sparkles fly and twist around the cloud. How come I'm not sneezing?

"You aren't in the spell this time," Aunt Heather tells me.

She and Karly are watching the sparkly smoke without even blinking. The smoke is gray. No, it's kind of like dirty dishwater. I tried to drink some once. Too soapy. Um, it's clearing up, water with sparkly bubbles in it.

I can see through it.

A monster, with a smooth, wide head about three times as big as mine, small, round eyes the size of my toes, no ears, and four of my bodies long, is curled around Joey. Sharp spikes are on top of the evil thing's head, and there are claws all over its skin, not just its feet. Actually, its legs end in stumps with claws. It doesn't look like he has feet. Logs with joints. That's what he walks on. He's lying down, so I can't tell how tall he is. Now I can smell the stinky Horrible Hodag. This time I sneeze and cough to clear my poor nose and mouth of the stench.

Lips pull into a snarl, and growling, I lunge for the monster. It has him! Joey is in real trouble. I hear Auntie Heather and Karly racing behind me. The Horrible Hodag is eating him.

"No! Stop it! You can't hurt my friend," Joey shouts at me, waving his arms to keep me back. What did The Horrible Hodag do to the Boypup? The Creep has always been strange, but this is a bit beyond that. I give him my best basset stare, while watching to make sure The Horrible Hodag doesn't do anything to hurt my Boypup. My Boypup, huh? I guess so. My Pack.

My sensitive ears hear Auntie Heather and Karly slowly creep behind me. 'Kay, I don't really need sensitive ears, Peeps are loud no matter how much they try to be quiet in the woods. At least my claws don't clatter on the leaves. Hmmm. I lift my paw and put it down again. All fixed, no pain. I can beat The Horrible Hodag.

"Grrrrarooorrrrrr. Snap! Grrrrr."

Game on monster.

"Joey, what are you doing with that…creature?" Auntie Heather asks, very softly.

"I told you, she's my friend. George, no, no, bad dog. You're scaring him."

Not likely. Steam is curling up from slits where its nose should be and its eyes are dark and spinning. Where are its ears? How can it smellhear anything? Its smell/taste makes me want to puke. Except then I'd have to take my eyes off of it.

"Grrrr."

Leave my Boypup alone you freak of nature. "Arrrroo!" I sound my battle cry and charge in for the kill. I stop short, my neck nearly pulled to my back. Auntie Heather has my leash under her foot.

Again.

What is wrong with that Boypup? I face the monster again. "Grrrr." Give my Boypup back, right now, or I'll eat you. "Grrr."

The Horrible Hodag moves a leg and shuffles Joey closer into him. Whatever was under them crackled. I crinkle my nose. Cheese puffs? Potato Chips? Would he share?

The monster growls at me.

Um. No, that isn't a growl. It's purring. Cats purr. Cats are monsters! "Grrrr." Back off from my Boypup, Horrible Hodag.

"Arooo. Arf. Barkbarkbarkbark."

"Auntie Heather, make George stop! He's scaring Chari," Joey The Creep says. He's a creep again. He's in the arms of a big, ugly cat.

I roll my eyes at Auntie Heather and continue challenging the monster. The Boypup is insane from the stench of the thing. Roquefort climbs down from his perch and crawls onto my back. I snap at him. What is he doing there? He puts his hands on my muzzle.

Karly takes my leash from under Auntie Heather's foot. I try to pull, but she's gotten strong. Must be the Wheaties. "How can she be your friend?" My Girlpup asks.

Roque chatters his teeth at me, lets me go, and paces near Auntie Heather. Did he just tell me off?

"She just is. I found this place. Stuff was all wrong. I felt all stuffy, like I had a cold. My eyes didn't work right. Then I fell into a hole. She flew down and got me. I coulda died an' no one else came when I yelled," The Creep whined. "I hurt my ankle an' she fixed me." He works his foot out from under the monster and wiggles it to show us. It's missing a shoe.

Oh, I believe that. The Horrible Hodag *fixed* him. No way can that thing heal anything. Well, at least that explains the shoe we found. The bed the monster and The Creep are on crunches with their movement. What are those? I strain my eyes. My nose is my main tool, vision isn't important. Smell/taste/feel is what it's all about. They look like bags. Of course! Potato chip bags. Cheese puff bags. Corn chip bags. The shiny kind of bag hard to tear. Shiny like aluminum foil food is cooked in. Lots and lots of bags.

I am jealous. Where did he get all the treasure? There aren't any crumbs on The Creep's face and he's a messy eater. The Horrible Hodag didn't share.

"Joey, can you come here? We won't hurt your friend, but your mom is very worried about you. There are a lot of people worried and they're looking for you. You don't want them to find your friend, do you? She's probably shy if she likes to hide," Auntie Heather says softly. As if she could scare the monster off if she talked normally. "Grrr." Let The Creep go. Karly and Auntie Heather give me "that" look. I break off my warning.

The Creep pets The Horrible Hodag, carefully stroking the sharp needles back, avoiding getting stabbed. The monster rubs its big head against the Boypup's chest. Like an ugly stupid cat. "Aroo!" *Cat*! The Hodag looks at me and draws her lips over pointy narrow teeth. I can show him teeth…

Karly pulls back on her leash. "You're not helping. If you can't be nice I'll…I'll… take you back to the car." As if she would. I have the power here. I growl again. She glares at me and pulls her leash toward the car.

I give her my patented "basset eyes." No one can resist them.

Except her.

She continues to pull, even though I dig in my rear paws.

"Karly, it's all right. Just keep him from looking the Hodag in the face. It just sets him off. Dog instincts are trumping his common sense. I think I know one reason why the Hodag is protecting your brother."

Roque climbs on my back—*again*—and puts his hands over my eyes. I shake, but he's sticking like a burr. Karly tightens her leash.

I'm trapped.

"The Hodag isn't protecting Joey." Karly sounds panicky. "He's trapped him."

If she'd let me go, I could do something to take her panic away. The link is still between us, but she is ignoring it. No. She's scared and not thinking about the bond. I lick my lips to appease her. She doesn't notice.

Or doesn't get it.

She needs to learn dog. She will learn dog if I have to bite her.

"I'm not trapped." Joey lifts The Horrible Hodag's paws from around his middle. How can he stand the smell/taste? Peeps have no senses at all. The Boypup stands up next to the monster and pets her head. Wait, The Boypup never pets my head like that.

"Karly, give me my shoe," The Creep demands, holding out his hand, feet planted.

My Girlpup tosses it to The Creep. A long tongue unrolls from behind the pointed teeth and snags the shoe.

"Hey, that's mine." The Boypup tries to get his shoe back from the monster. The Horrible Hodag peels it off her tongue with his paw and tucks it into the wrappers. There are other things in there as well. All sorts of shiny things—chains, cans, foil balls. More. I can't smell/taste if there is anything good baked on the foil. Sometimes there is. I can't smell anything except for gassulfurdrysnakecatstink. I look at my Packmates. Why don't they smell/taste its grossness? Peeps. Said it before, and I'll say it again: Peeps, no common senses.

Maybe there are chips in one of the bags? I try to pull closer. Karly pulls me back. I need to put a collar on her. See if she likes having her neck yanked around. It's not my fault I can't hold onto her leash. She doesn't need to jerk me around. It's like the leash is for me or something.

The Horrible Hodag puts a big paw back around the Boypup and…it looks like it's snuggling him in. No way. No way is that monster snuggling with my Packmate. "Arfffaroooarrrg."

Auntie Heather steps closer to them. "Joey, I think I know what your friend wants. She's like a magpie. There are stories that dragons hoard shiny things. That's what it looks like she's doing."

Joey kicks his feet and tries to get The Horrible Hodag's front legs off him. "Stop it. I want my shoe. I want to go home now. I'm hungry." He stops kicking. "What's a magpie?"

"It's a bird that likes to collect shiny things and hide them. Everything in that pile you're on is shiny." Auntie Heather rubs under her chin. "In fact, you're shiny. Can you slide off the helmet and your other shoe?"

"I don't wanna." The Boypup turns to his "friend." "Let me go. I want to go home." I recognize that look. He's about to pitch a fit. I eye the monster. It might eat him. I would if I was a monster and Joey was acting like that. The smell/taste of the Peeps' bones rolls through my mouth. I shake out the thought. Note to self: never make a joke like that again.

Must think.

I sit and scratch an itch on my chin with a rear paw. What to do? I keep scratching until I'm afraid my Packmates are going to think I have fleas. Then they'll give me an awful bath with pennyroyal.

Ick.

"Puff the magic dragon," Auntie Heather murmurs.

Was that an old familiar of hers? I've never seen a dragon.

Shudder.

If they look like this I'm glad I haven't. How could Auntie Heather live with one?

"I'm betting the Hodag only wants the shiny helmet and maybe the shoes." Aunt Heather whispers. I don't think it was for us. "Joey, slide off your shoe and remove your helmet. Drop them on the pile as a present to your new friend."

"But they're mine. Mom won't let me ride my bike without my helmet and my tennies are new," The Creep is whining. I hate it when he whines. My ears feel like one of the Hodag's needles is piercing it.

"I promise, we'll get you new ones. See her nest?" Auntie Heather points to the not very-interesting-garbage pile. "See how much she likes bright sparkly things? She'll like your gift and she won't miss you so much."

Snort.

More like he won't miss you.

Auntie Heather looks back at me. I return with patented basset "innocent" eyes.

"When she lets you go, we'll get you home for dinner. Your mother is very upset that she couldn't find you."

Joey bites his lower lip. He does it when he's thinking something over.

"Is she mad at me? I don't wanna be grounded." He looks at the paw wrapped around his tummy.

"She's understandably worried. You didn't come home or call her to tell her you'd be late. We'll tell her the truth; you made an important new friend. Your mom will understand. Now, can you remove your helmet and shoe?"

Roque bends toward the Boypup and Horrible Hodag and makes a crooning sound. As if that will make anything better.

Joey wiggles his foot. The shoe bounces off a hubcap and lights up. The Horrible Hodag whips out a forked tail and scuffs the shoe closer to his front paws. He settles his head on it and tucks my Boypup closer to his chest. He purrs.

"Grrr." That worked well, didn't it? I lick my front paw. Roque and I can rush her. The monster will chase us and Joey can escape. I growl low in my throat.

Karly grabs my collar and shakes me a little. Fine. You do it. You rush in and save Joey.

"Stop it. Give Auntie Heather a chance."

Why does Karly only use our mind link when she wants to?

"When you take off your helmet, toss it further away. She needs to let you go before we can get you."

Joey nods to Auntie Heather and I know what to do. Wish I could tell Roque to follow my lead.

My Boypup undoes the strap under his chin and pulls the helmet off with his free hand. Boypup's more coordinated than I gave him credit for. He flings it at me.

Nice.

Missed.

Creep.

Just when I'm starting to like…

The Horrible Hodag unwraps from around Joey, stretches front legs to back, and then lopes over to the helmet.

I back up and slide my head out of the collar. Always a useful trick. I rush in and grab the Boypup by his collar. Roque is pushing him from behind. Joey struggles until he sees his "friend" coming back. Joey's tummy rumbles and mine rumbles back in sympathy. His tummy wins. He stops fighting us and runs to Auntie Heather. She catches him on the fly. Both of them almost land on the ground from the impact. My Boypup is growing up.

Wings pop out of the side of the monster. She looks from Joey to her pile of useless trash. I decide there is nothing tasty there. She makes a creakyrustygate sound and goes back to bed. She gives us all a hard unblinking stare, turns around a few times, smushing down the garbage, and settles in with her shiny toy.

White fogcloud streams from her nose.

"Aroo!" We need to get out now! Nownownow! Must keep my Pack safe. I dance around, better at herding everyone away from the danger than a border collie.

Chapter Eighteen

We run as if the fogcloud is following us out of woods. A quick scan shows it's not, but I don't trust magic fogclouds.

Um. Where is everyone else?

"George, the Hodag has no interest in us. You don't need to run away," says my auntie with a laugh.

Huff, huff, huff.

I'm not running away. I'm worried about my Pack and want to show them the way to safety. I slow my pace anyway. They could've gotten lost. I have superior senses and never get lost. Yep, that's it. Basset hounds may not be built for speed, but we can sprint when necessary. Like when game is getting away.

"Surrrre that's it," Karly draws out the sure. She's using our link against me. "Come here and give me your head. You can't be without your collar and leash when we see the police."

I amble over to my Girlpup and raise my head so she can put my collar on. I admit, I feel naked when it's not on. She snaps her leash to the ring and my Pack and I walk to the parking lot.

Auntie Heather must've called the police earlier because all the Peeps that were looking for The Cre…Joey are in the parking lot. They shout and stampede over when they notice us. I strut, with my head held high. Yep, I found the Boypup. It's my duty to protect my Pack.

They pass Joey around. He doesn't like the attention and squirms away the best he can.

Finally Packdad and Packmom are able to get through. Packdad picks the Boypup up and spins him around.

"Aw Dad, don't do that. The guys can see us."

Packdad stops spinning, but doesn't put him down. Packmom puts a hand on Joey's face and kisses him. Packmom and Packdad are hugging, with Joey struggling to get free between them.

"Where have you been all day? Why didn't you call me?" she scolds him and then kisses him. So wrong. Kissing scent marks someone is yours, a part of the Pack. Peeps kisses are usually too dry. Useless. No wonder why Peeps don't know who belongs to what.

"What happened?" she finally asks.

This should be good. I sit and watch, comfy, slouching on one hip.

"Nothin'. I found a friend and we played. I'm sorry. Can we eat now? I'm hungry."

Makes two of us. I give patented "basset eyes." No one notices. Sigh.

Packmom eyes Auntie with a cocked head.

"That would be about right. We found him safe with a new friend." Auntie Heather stresses "new friend" and the Packparents look confused. No surprise. I've been confused since we found The Horrible Hodag didn't have the Boypup for dinner.

The Badge Dude pushes though the crowd. He ruffles Joey's hair. How can the Boypup stand that? Ick. I want to shake my own fur into place in sympathy.

"You caused your parents a lot of worry today little man. We searched every inch of this park and couldn't find you anywhere. You're lucky your dog was able to lead your aunt and sister to you. Why didn't you call?"

Wait a minute?

Whose dog?

As if.

Joey looks between the Badge Dude and the Packparents. He stretches out to his full height. Only about three of me tall. He needs to grow. "I'm eight and a big boy. See, I'm fine. 'Sides, my friend wanted to look at my phone. I tried to call, but it didn't work after she licked it."

Augh. That's just gross. The monster *licked* the phone? Apparently, the group agreed. Their eyes were huge, round, and white, the way they get when they hear something unexpected.

The Badge Peep clears his throat. "Where's your friend? I'd like to talk to her."

"She's hiding. She's shy." Joey struggles and slides to the ground. "Can we go home now? I'm starving to death," he whines.

Aroo! Yes! Time to eat! I get up and dance in circles. It's supp/supp/supper/time/time.

Badge Dude bends to get closer to Joey. "Why is she hiding? Where are her parents?"

"She doesn't have any. Mom, puhleeeeeze can we go get dinner. Puhleeeeeze?" The Boypup tugs Packmom's shirt.

Auntie Heather puts a hand on the Boypup's shoulder and looks down at the Badge Dude. She has shiny eyes and a goofy smile on her face. Ack! Spring! The dance continues. Wrong, but they don't seem to notice they're missing the important steps. Heck, they won't even let me sniff crotches and butts and that's the best way to get to know someone. They don't even have the body language right.

For example: their ears can't move to show their interest, they don't have tails, and rarely wag their butts. They only have smiles, which mean a lot of things, and shiny eyes. Which could be from allergies.

"I didn't see Joey with anyone Officer James. He was curled up, sleeping in a pile of leaves. Poor guy was exhausted from hiking in the woods." She pats Joey on the back.

"Was not! You saw! I was with…"

"Your invisible friend. Yes, of course you were." Auntie Heather winks at the Badge Dude. "Very smart kids have special friends. I think we've all had enough excitement for the day, don't you, Doreen?"

Packmom gives Auntie Heather a confused look. "Yes. Um, yes. I'd like to get Joey home. He's had a very busy day. Thanks so much, everyone, for helping find my son. I don't know what…" Packmom sniffles a little.

"Go home. We'll get in touch with you if there any questions." The Badge Dude turns to the crowd.

"Thank you everyone. It makes my job much easier when the community pitches in to help as you all did." Badge Dude heads for his car.

The crowd breaks up, some stopping over to give the Boypup a kiss, a hug, a pinch on the cheek, or a scolding.

There should be more scolding and less petting. Why would the Boypup run off with a monster and call it his friend? I wouldn't have thought the Boypup would like girls yet. Hmmm. It is spring. Ick. I shake my head at the stupidity of Boypups and follow the Packparents to the car.

Auntie Heather is talking to them. Blah blah blah, nothing worth listening to. Lived through it. Chapter done.

The Boypup should go without dinner. Since I am the hero, Packmom should give me his share. I drool and lick my lips. Peeps' food is tasty.

Kibble is nummy, but Peeps' food is for special occasions. I'm sure saving the Boypup from The Horrible Hodag is a special occasion.

In the meantime, if they're going to yap outside the car, I'm going to sleep. With a yawn, I circle the magic three times and make myself comfy on the ground. I use Karly's foot for a pillow.

She won't mind.

My eyes barely close before Karly pulls her foot out and toes my side.

Oof.

What is that for?

"We're going blockhead. Can you get into the car or do you need a boost?" She smell/tastes impatienthungrytired. The back door is open. The Boypup is sitting in *my* seat, shotgun. I hop into the rear and plaster my face against the window. "Roo," I speak softly. I get yelled at if I'm loud.

Packmom is in the driver's seat. She twists around to see me. "Heather told me it isn't safe to let your head hang out. You could get something in your eyes. Sorry, no ears flapping in the wind for you."

How unfair. I love the smell/tastes as they blow through my cheeks and ears. The feeling of speed and power. I'm all for energy saving, but it doesn't mean I can't enjoy it when it's someone else's.

"You need to move George. I need some room back here." Packdad pushes me to the middle. Now there is no space for me. I push my nose under Karly's legs and kick my rear paws out to make room. Karly lifts her legs. Packdad pulls me onto his lap.

Sigh.

That works for me.

The smell/taste of The Horrible Hodag fills the car. The Boypup is covered in it. No way can I go home filling my mouth and nose. Pfffffffart. Long. Low. Pleasing. Now the car smell/tastes right.

Everyone yells. The windows open.

Chapter Nineteen

"Spill it. What really happened?" I don't like it when drivers aren't looking at the road. I see Packmom's face in the rearview mirror. She's driving safely. Phew. Funny, that's the sound everyone made before.

The Boypup is snoring. He couldn't wait until we made the five-minute trip home. He's wasting the good seat. I feel queasy. It's my Kryptonite, my great weakness. I get carsick unless I can see out the front. I know there are plants to keep my stomach down, but who knew the Boypup was going to take my spot. He could've at least let me sit on his lap.

Packmom sighs. "Karly, what happened back there?"

Oh no. Maybe the Boypup has a point. I plop across my Pack's laps and take a pup-nap until we get home. Been there, done that, don't need to remember my awesomeness in fighting for the Boypup. Karly'll tell Packmom how wonderful I was and I'll get a super supper. Snorksnorksnor…

The car isn't moving anymore. The doors creak open and legs move and slide out. I drop myself out after them. You know, if they're going to make me go in a metal box on wheels, they could at least make it lower to make it easier to get in and out.

I am ready for my Peep food. My tail spins and I drool. I amble to the door and follow my Pack in. Feed me already! I'm a hero! Give me my reward.

"Go get cleaned up, Karly, Joey, I'll get dinner warmed up." Packmom turns to Packdad and hugs and kisses him. Hey, no kissing, it's time for dinner! Stop wasting time. "I was sure he was gone." She slumps into a chair. I smell/taste the fearhormone push through her skin. Time for Superbasset. I sit on her foot and put a paw on her lap.

"I'll get food out in a minute." She looks at me and strokes my head.

"Hon, I'll do it." Packdad almost steps on me as he bends over to kiss her on the head. I turn to lick her hand, just to show him how it's done. She smell/tastes saltysweet, not so scared.

"I don't understand how there can be a dragon in the park. However, ever since I married into your family, I've discovered I don't understand a lot of things. Heather will solve the problem. Actually, she didn't seem as concerned when she brought Joey out." He kisses her again and backs away.

Hey, don't forget *who* brought Joey out. And, would it hurt you to give me a scritch? I flip over and present my tummy. Packdad gives me a quick rub, gets up, goes to the place that all the food comes from, and gets out bowls of the stuff.

"Is it okay if I just zap it in the microwave?" he asks, as he peels off the tops and looks inside each bowl. I go over to him and cock my head. You can drop a little here. I'll make sure it's all clean.

"Hmmm? Oh, yes, that'll be fine. What do you mean, Heather seemed less concerned?" Packmom stops petting me and gets up to clatter plates around.

"She wasn't as tense. Maybe it was because she found Joey. Or maybe she knows what's going on with that dragon. She's your sister, you need to ask her about it. I'd like Heather's take on it. Sometimes it's hard to know what Karly saw versus what she thought she saw. Granted, it's not every day that anyone sees dragons."

"Hodag. Heather said it was a Hodag."

Beep. Beep. Beep.

Whine.

The microwave is telling us it's time to eat. I watch Packdad as he gets all the wonderful food. It smell/tastes wheatycookedcowtomatogreen. Oh nummy. Packmom made spaghetti and meatballs. I bump her leg to remind her I get my share.

"Hmmm. What do you want?" Packmom looks at me with a smile. As if she doesn't know. I sit and drool. Get up and walk to my supper dish and drool in it.

"I suppose you think you should get a special treat for your part in saving Joey? Here." She scoops a blob of spaghetti and meatballs into my bowl.

Oh, heaven.

Just heaven.

The smell/tastes swirl up, tickling my tongue. I can't wait. My nose deep into the bowl, I slurp the lovely stuff down.

It's gone.

I look around.

Behind.

I slide my bowl to look under it.

Where did my food go? "NoooOOOooooowoowoo."

"You've had your share. Might want to wipe your muzzle, though. There's red sauce all over it. Looks like you got into a fight with some…" Packmom's voice breaks off into a whimper. Why? Spaghetti doesn't fight.

"Shush. It's okay. Joey's fine. Heather and her friends will get to the bottom of this."

Peeps, it's over. Worry about now, not before. Before is gone, nothing to do about it. Like the spaghetti.

Loud thunks come from the other room before Joey crashes into the room. "Is dinner ready yet." Joey bounces like a ball. Crazy Peep.

"Yes, it is. Sit down. Where's Karly?" Packmom asks.

"Coming, Mom. Is George there?"

"There's food here, where else would he be?"

Hey, I'm not a stupid familiar. However, I am a sleepy one. I know from experience no one is going to share with me, and since the Boypup got older, no one drops anything either. Doesn't stop me from walking around the table and drooling on laps as food is passed around. They ignore me. I make my three spins and collapse on the rug next to the sink.

Something nudges my paw. I shake it off. A foot pushes under my belly.

"Come on big guy, my turn to do dishes, but you need to get out of the way." Packdad adds in a whisper, "If you're good there might be something in it for you."

Oh boy. Yum! Leftovers. I am always good. My tail thumps on the floor and I smile.

Oh.

I check the room to see if Karly is around. I suppose I should find out what she's doing.

Except.

Spaghetti leftovers.

I'm torn.

She can't get into too much trouble. It was only a short cat…erm, dog nap.

It's *spaghetti* leftovers.

My drool pools on the floor.

Packdad bends over with a rag and wipes it up. "I guess I better scrape the plates before I slip on your puddles. Hard to believe I was more concerned about the puddles from your other end when Heather first brought you over." He chuckles.

Very funny. I haven't had an accident since…well, it was a long time ago. No reason to bring it up. I'd glare, but the smell/taste of spaghetti in a bowl clacking in front of me keeps my eyes down.

Score.

Packmom's voice and footsteps get louder as she comes closer to the kitchen. As a predator I notice important things like this. I'm not supposed to eat from the Peeps dishes and they aren't supposed to eat from mine. I scarf down the remaining bits of noodles. There is a little green tree left on the bowl. I munch on it thoughtfully. Not as tasty as carrots, but not bad.

"Heather, one sec. Brian, George's bowl is in the corner. Would it've been too much to scrape the scraps into it? Honestly. What? Yes, he's the culprit. I know, we're supposed to cut back on George's food." She looks at Packdad. "Did you hear that? No more food for George unless it's scheduled."

Auntie Heather's voice sounds underwater on the phone. I don't get how Peeps can use the things, but, whatever. My hearing is much better than any Peep's.

Packdad answers with a funny smile. "You have it on speaker, I think the kids can hear it from upstairs. Hey, you're the one that gave him a bowl first."

Packmom sighs. "No more…So, Heather, the Hodag is a friendly dragon? How can that be? Karly said he, I mean she, wouldn't let Joey go. What about the bones?"

"Can you come out tomorrow with us? I have a good idea what's going on. I'd like to get your take on it, though."

"Yes, of course. You're sure that the kids aren't going to be hurt by this thing?" I keep dodging Packmom's feet as she paces the length of the kitchen. Packdad puts a hand on her shoulder and leads her to a chair. Good, I was worried about my tail. I swipe my tongue over it. Pee time. I dance to the door.

"Hang on, George. Can't you wait until she's off the phone? I need to know what's going on."

Packdad is scolding me for this? Whatever they're saying won't change in three seconds. It's potty time—that's what's important. I scratch the door and cross my legs to keep everything in. Hurry up! A fart booms from behind me. I look at Packdad. He looks at me. Whoa. Who knew I live with a pro? Wonder if he gives lessons.

He shakes his head and waves his hands in the air. "You win. Let's get you out before I have more to clean up."

The leash is hanging on the door. It seems strange to me that he has to use it. After all, he's old enough to know the neighborhood. With a snap, we're connected and out the door. I race to my spot and whizz away. Not enough time to check pee-mail or add any new messages. Whew. Sigh. Thank goodness. I check for a good spot and do my business, and wait for Packdad to clean up after me.

We dash back to the house. Packmom is sitting at the table, looking at her phone.

"Heather is certain we don't have to worry about anything right now. She'll explain tomorrow. Why don't you go watch a movie with the kids and I'll make some popcorn. Joey needs a little family time. Even if he doesn't think anything special happened, I'm still a little weirded out. *I* need a little family time."

Packdad strokes her hair. Hey, hello, you're supposed to do that for me.

"I'll make the popcorn, go be with the kids." He kisses her and helps her out of her seat. Pulls her into his arms. Kisses her on those strange lips. Pushes her toward the family room. Peeps are very strange.

Since he burns more popcorn than he makes, I follow Packmom to check on my Girlpup. It was a crazy day, even for a witchlet.

Chapter Twenty

"I've got hot cinnamon rolls," Auntie Heather calls out as she walks into the house. "Is there hot water for tea?" She's carrying a box and a bag. She puts the bag on the table.

"It's Tuesday, it's early in the morning, and there's a dragon out there. Why are you so happy?" Packdad wonders over his coffee mug.

I like coffee. It smell/tastes good. Sweetmilkbittersharp. They never share any with me though. I drink it from the bottom of their mugs when they leave them on the short tables.

Packdad lifts his nose and sucks in smell/taste. He's loud. Peeps have no idea how to use their noses. "I might forgive you for walking in so cheerful. Did you make them this morning?"

Auntie Heather pulls one out of the box and places it on the plate Packdad used for his toast. I wanted to lick the crumbs. I can wait for cinnamon roll crumbs. I drool. Or maybe a cinnamon roll. My Packpups could drop one.

"Not happening. I brought over some dried yams for you. Yes, I thought it would be easier to explain what's happening in the park over something sweet." Auntie Heather reaches into her bag and tosses a piece of bark at me. It doesn't smell/taste like bark. I pick it up and chew it. Nice. Crunchy with a sweetstarch smell/taste that finishes with spicy cinnamon. I gulp it and wag for another. Auntie Heather tosses me a half.

Crunch.

She gives me "that" look. "No more for you. I also want to see if I can borrow Karly for the day again. It's for a unique learning experience."

"She's upstairs with the Joey. They should be down in"—he looks at his watch—"two, three, four…"

Trucks are lighter on the road than my Packpups going down stairs. They rush into the kitchen and each grab a roll. I give them my best "basset eyes." They ignore me. How rude. They run to the family room to watch the box with no smell/taste or smell/feel. Just sound and sight. Nothing useful about it.

Packmom pushes her hair back and pulls a chair out from the table. She settles in with her hands on the table and her head on her hands. Packdad pours her some coffee.

With cream and sugar.

I want some. They ignore me. What is with this family?

"So what are we going to do about the dragon?" Packdad asks.

"I told you last night, the Hodag isn't dangerous. Go to work, we'll call you if we need you for anything," Auntie Heather says, taking a roll for herself and sitting down.

Packmom eyes the rolls. She gets up and grabs two plates, sliding one to Auntie Heather, and putting a roll on one for herself. She takes a bite and gets a funny look on her face. I know that look. I creep over to where she's sitting and put my head on her lap. I look at the table leg. I was very artistic when I was teething as a pup. A hand thumps on my nose as Packmom slips the roll to me. I gulp it down. Packmom can be picky about what she eats. We make a good team and no one gets his feelings hurt.

When I crawl out from under the table, Auntie Heather stares at me. Uh oh. Busted. Hey, not my fault the roll fell into my mouth.

Auntie Heather shakes her head and continues talking to Packdad. "You'll just get in the way. It would be far easier if you didn't come. Take Joey with you, pretend it's 'take your kid to work' day. He'll love being with you."

Packdad folds his hands on the table. "Tell me what that creature is and why you think it's safe and I'll think about not tagging along. I'm not forgetting the human bones George found."

"The Hodag only comes out when the woods are in trouble. She guards and protects that land. The last time she was out, according to the book, was one hundred years ago when a farmer tried to cut down all the trees. She shared the prairie, but those woods are sacred to her kind. When she came out, she marked the borders using her..." Auntie Heather does something weird with her hands, lifting them in the air and bending two fingers a few times. That is a new Peep body language word to me. "...'fiery breath to scorch the trees'. It took a while to figure out the writing since it was mixed with drawings. Things also started to go missing along with sightings of a dragon. The Indians in the area told him that the spirit of the woods didn't want him trespassing. That's when the will was written. The will we must find somehow."

Auntie Heather bites into her roll, chews and swallows without sharing with me. "Besides, those bones had nothing to do with the Hodag. I figured out where they came from last night."

"They came from a person. That's all I need to know."

"Of course they came from a person. It's just that the Hodag didn't murder the person. In fact, nobody was murdered." Auntie Heather reaches for her bag and pulls out two bones and a coil of dark wire.

"Heather!" Packmom shrieks. "Those. Are. Human. Bones. They don't belong on my table. That's disgusting," Packmom eyes the pile and turns her head.

"What? They're not dirty. Give them proper respect, Doreen. They may be bones, but they were once a person." She takes the old wire I remember her finding in the pit, and sticks an end into the bone. It slides in like a rope through a tennis ball. I used to like to chase and play tug when I was a silly pup. She strings the other bone to the first and holds them by the wire. They make an arm. A Peep's arm. Peeps' arms belong under skin, not just hanging there. Although, it does look like a toy. I want to get a better sniff. Auntie Heather stops me with a glance.

"These used to be part of a whole skeleton that hung in a doctor's office a very long time ago. I have no clue how the Hodag got it, but the wire was probably shiny and attracted her. She loves shiny things and now she seems happy with shiny chip bags. The Hodag isn't dangerous—she hasn't hurt anyone. There's absolutely no need for you to come with us. In fact, you'll just get in the way." Auntie Heather puts the bone and the wire back in her bag.

Packdad taps his fingers on the table. "Nice story. Good to know she's a 'spirit.' Still not happening. I'm coming with. How do you know it's not going to protect the woods against you? I'll watch Joey, but I'm staying close by in case you need me. These are my kids and there's a monster out there. I'm not about to go off to work and leave my family while you go do something witchy and hope you can make it go away."

That might have been a great speech, if Packdad's mouth wasn't filled. It puzzles me that Packmom didn't want hers. Well, her loss, my gain. I look over at her, hope springing eternal. She is looking at the Packpups walking into the kitchen.

"I'm coming too. You aren't hurting my friend," the Boypup sticks out his lower lip.

Got to give it to the boy, he's loyal.

Almost as loyal as a dog.

Auntie Heather leaves the table and crouches by the Boypup. "We aren't going to hurt her. She's a good friend to have, but we need to fix some things so she's happy. You can help by staying with your dad and keeping an eye on him. Can you do that?"

"I want to see her." He turns to Packdad. "Dad? You going to meet my friend, too? Otherwise I'm going with Auntie Heather." Lip still out. If he were a dog, his rear paws would be digging into the ground. He wasn't going with Packdad unless he could show him his new friend.

Foolish Boypup.

"Men." Aunt Heather says under her breath. With my outstanding ears, it's easy to hear her. "Fine. We need to get to the woods. I think I know what you two can do. Brian, make sure you have your phone."

"The van is big enough for all of us, if you want to come with us." Packmom grabs keys from the counter. Packdad, thin and as fast as a gray whippet, tries to take them from her. "Uh-uh, my van, I get to drive."

"We're not going to drive. No chemical smells on us. We do need to wash up before we go." Auntie Heather rummages in her bag again. "Use this soap, I made it, should be natural enough, I should think."

I look at her, round-eyed. I am not taking a bath. I am a natural creature and don't stink of chemicals.

"You're fine as you are George. Hurry up everyone. We have a Hodag to take care of."

Chapter Twenty-One

It's a mystery to me that Joey is never leashed. Karly always is when we're outside. Personally, I think she's outgrown the need. Then again, I don't want to be his keeper.

Joey is hopping around like a rabbit, asking a gazillion questions. I stop listening. He's a creepy pest and better not get in the way of our work. I trot —a basset on a mission.

We look like a parade going down the road. Packmom, Packdad, and Auntie Heather with Roque are in the front. Karly and I are sandwiched in the middle, and The Boypup is boinging around like prey. I'm sort of surprised the Hodag didn't decide to hunt and eat him. I guess it's good they made friends, though it seemed more like the dragon thought she owned him.

Auntie Heather is digging in her bag again as we walk.

Multitasking.

She rummages around and pulls out a notebook.

"Brian, if you want to be useful, can you make a few calls for me? I have a few questions that I hope these people can answer. By the time I was finished with my research last night it was too late to bother them. The list is on the page I dog-eared."

I stop. Dog-eared?

"Relax George. It means I folded the corner down."

Packdad takes the notebook. "I'm afraid to ask, but do you really understand George?"

"I've shared my life with a lot of animals. I've learned a little about how they think over the years," Auntie Heather says with a smile to Roque and me.

Yeah, as if.

She's in my mind.

"Back to the list. I might be on the wrong track. There are probably a bunch of things I've missed, so if you think of anything else, please add them. This isn't something I've had any experience with. I wasn't even sure where to start."

Packdad takes the notebook from her. She couldn't just tell him what she wants to know? What if the notebook gets wet or something? It'll be just like what happened to the magical cookbook. The notebook doesn't smell/taste good enough to fix it with drool. Plus, if she told him, I'd hear what was on the pages. I want to know but I can't read it. Sometimes Peeps are so frustrating! Most of the time, come to think about it.

Packdad opens the notebook, wrinkles his forehead, and grins. "This might just work. I have some friends that might also be able to help."

"What? What might work?" Packmom stops him and looks at the paper. She grins as well. "Is this true?"

"Guess we'll find out. I'll make the calls. Except…if you run into trouble how will I know? Can't you wait until I'm done?" Packdad asks Auntie Heather as he pulls out his phone.

"Put that away. *No* chemical smells on us. And that's why you can't come. We don't want to irritate the Hodag with the smells of civilization." Auntie Heather sounds a bit irritated. Well, she didn't tell anyone why they had to clean up.

She must realize she was wrong because she arches an eyebrow. It's very expressive. Peeps are sadly lacking in body language skills, but this is a good one. I copy the move. Yup. I'm better at it.

"If I think there is any chance we're going to have a problem, I'll send George or Roque back for you. The Hodag is only protecting her territory. Once she knows it's safe, she'll go back into hibernation or whatever Hodags do when they aren't needed."

"There are other Hodags?" Karly asks. I'm glad she does, I want to know.

"Must be. There are a lot of dragon stories around the world. Brian, I assume you agree to make the calls?"

Packdad runs fingers through his hair. I wish I could do that. Scratching is good and all, but the bliss of my own fingers…What am I thinking? Peeps' fingers *are* mine. "I'm trusting you with my family, Heather, against my better judgment, but yes. If anything at all seems off, even a pebble that shouldn't be there, you send George back to me."

"Of course," Auntie Heather says. Under her breath she says, in a voice only my amazing basset hearing can pick up, "As if he could do anything useful."

She does a lot of murmuring. Peeps' smellhearing is useless.

"Doreen, Karly, George, let's go talk to a Hodag. Good luck Brian." Auntie Heather calls us together and we march into the woods looking for a monster.

Chapter Twenty-Two

The fogcloud is further into the woods today. Karly is shivering. I guess it is a little chilly for a human with naked skin. Human design flaw, they are full of them. I look up. Is it colder because the shade is deeper here?

No.

The whole woods is made up of trees. It's the fogcloud. The animals are still missing. I sniff, tongue hanging from my mouth. Not even a crumb of rabbit smell/taste.

I drag my paws. The Hodag is bad, no matter what Auntie Heather thinks. The dragon scared away everything that lives here. There isn't even the whinebite of a mosquito. Huh. That isn't such a bad thing. Yes it is. Birds eat them. I chase birds. There is nothing good about The bad Hodag. It smell/tastes bad. It sleeps on a tasteless trash pile, and it tried to steal the Boypup. I look at Packmom. She'd miss him.

The smell/taste of gassulfurdrysnakecatstink races through my mouth and nose, before it bullets into my brain. It's beyond awful. What is wrong with my Peeps? Why aren't they covering their noses and running away? Roque looks as disgusted as I am.

Why do I even ask? What do I expect from them? They rub chemicals all over to mask their natural odor. As if that will hide them from their prey. Not that they could find any.

As we get closer the fogcloud recognizes we are superior and backs off. I stand straight, up on my toes, and growl low. Coward.

The fogcloud is gone. The Horrible Hodag is nested in her pile of shiny garbage in front of us. She looks at me and shakes her tail. The spikes at the end of her tail rattle.

A warning.

My hackles go up.

My own warning.

Karly pulls the leash tight. Spoilsport. I glare at her from over my shoulder. I could take the dragon on.

I know I could.

"Stop it right now." Auntie Heather snaps at me. She faces the monster. "You aren't going to hurt anyone, are you, sweetie?" she croons.

Oh, barf.

It's a full-grown, fire-breathing dragon and she's treating it like an overgrown puppy. I sit hard on the ground, cock my hip, and look away in disgust. If she wants to be dragon food, I'm not watching.

Lunch? Did someone say lunch? Did we have lunch yet? My tummy makes a little bubbly noise. I'm hungry, but not lunchtime.

My tummy alarm hasn't gone off.

Karly gives a quick tug on the leash. I'm forced to look behind me. Auntie Heather is walking to the monster, holding out a shiny pop can. Roque is biting his claws. I smellfeel the worry coming off him. He probably is picking up mine as well. Karly is excited.

The Hodag's eyes sparkle. She rolls to her feet, crackling trash the only sound in the woods. That's just wrong. Auntie Heather stops and waits while the dragon slithers like a snake on her belly. Why doesn't she use her legs? Hodags are built way wrong. Totally flawed.

Auntie Heather offers the back of her hand to sniff. Like that Horrible Hodag was a dog! I think about closing my eyes, positive the monster is going to bite Auntie Heather's hand off. No screams. Karly and I let out our breaths. No wonder I'm light headed.

The dragon leans into Auntie Heather and snurffles her hand, neck, and ear. Auntie Heather is a very brave witch.

Or a very stupid one.

She cooks really well, so she isn't stupid.

The dragon nudges Auntie Heather's hand as she takes the can into her paw. The ugly monster head tilts to my auntie. Horrible Hodag speak for "thank you"? Nyah, the thing isn't that smart. Auntie Heather is rubbing the Hodag's throat and cheeks.

"If the woods are saved, will you bring all the animals back? It isn't good for the woods to be without her children," Auntie Heather says. Ha. The Hodag surely can't understa…It makes a funny squawking nose, the first sound it's made. Coincidence. Has to be. Yeah, It's a trash-collecting monster. It can't be smart enough to talk. Besides, how would Auntie Heather know Hodag-speak?

She shoots me "that" look.

Well.

Um.

Okay.

Maybe.

Guess she can. I look away.

I turn my face forward again when a sound like rusty door hinges forced to open comes from the dragon. The monster tilts its head left. Then right.

Is it nearsighted?

"The woods and all that live here were always protected by you? I totally understand. So the animals are all safe?"

Auntie Heather got a lot more out of that head tilt and squawk than I did. How does she do that? When we aren't convincing a Horrible Hodag to go away, I'm going to find out. Education is important, after all. Even for a brilliant basset familiar.

The Horrible Hodag opens her mouth. It's awful, a ball splitting in half. Lining the halves are rows of sharp spikes that match the ones on her head and tail. They probably stick in what she eats like the ones on her head. Maybe they are poisonous. Maybe she's lying and she ate all the animals.

Auntie Heather whips around to me, puts her hands on her hips and stabs me with her eyes. "George, if you don't stop being so mean I swear you'll never see another treat again? Do you understand me?"

She's treating me like a puppy!

Um.

What did she say?

I freeze.

No.

More.

Treats?

My ears shoot up and my eyes grow wide. I don't understand what's going on, but I understand punishments. Can they both understand my thoughts? I try thinking of tuna fudge.

Cookies.

Rabbits. Rabbits. Where *are* the rabbits?

Oh yeah. Um. Oops. Tuna fudge. Biscuits...

"We'll get this fixed." Auntie Heather gestures to the path out. Roque climbs up to his seat on her shoulder. When we're almost to the parking lot she crosses her fingers. "I hope Brian was able to get some answers."

Chapter Twenty-Three

Packdad runs to us. "What happened? Did you find it? Is everyone safe?" He doesn't even take a breath between words. He grabs Packmom by the arms. If they kiss I'll leave. I'm about to trot off when he crouches to stroke my back. Guess he wants to check us all out. I lean into him. He stops with the petting action and steps away so I have to catch myself. Hey, warn a dog when you're going to move.

The Boypup is still jumping around. Auntie Heather must've put some sort of spell to keep him with Packdad. It's the only explanation. I wasn't that silly as a pup. Even then I knew it wasn't dignified for a basset.

"Which is why you kept getting tangled in your ears when you ran and slipped on the kitchen floor?"

Karly made that up. She stares at me like I'm nuts. "Admit it, you kind of like Joey."

Yeah, I'd miss him. He's part of the Pack, after all.

"Please, please, please tell me you found the will," Auntie Heather pleads. She's doing the potty dance, swaying from foot to foot. Roque scolds her and climbs down.

Packdad is looking at his phone. What is so interesting there? "I think I know what happened, if that helps. It's going to take a few days to…"

Auntie Heather rudely interrupts him. "I made a promise that we have to keep. Today. We have to fix this before the equipment does any more damage to the woods. The Hodag gave us a warning by scorching those trees. She marked as far as she'll allow the damage to go. She has weapons and I doubt she'll hold back using them to protect what's hers." She takes a breath. "Where do you think the will is?"

Roque waves to Auntie Heather. She nods and he takes off toward the house. He doesn't like being around too many people. Or maybe he's getting nummies. I want to go. Karly pulls back on her leash. What a time for her to accept our link. I try to close it. It's a smooth silver line between us, no clasp, with no way to break it. How was I supposed to know once she accepted it we'd be permanently bonded?

"Chill," my Girlpup insists. "I want to hear what's going on."

I slide to one hip and watch my Peeps. Oh, yeah. The will thing must be what was on the paper Auntie Heather gave to Packdad.

"No. Those were questions to help find the will."

Packmom looks around and then faces Auntie Heather. "Who are you talking to?"

"Karly. I let you and Brian read the list without sharing it with her. I forget she's growing up."

She never forgets anything. Auntie Heather didn't want me to know. Probably because I could've figured it out, and then Packdad wouldn't have anything to do.

Packmom still looks confused. I don't blame her. "I didn't hear…"

"We need to speed this up somehow. What can we do? Where do they think it is?"

"Tom is a history teacher at Karly's school…"

Karly groans. Packdad frowns at her.

"As I was saying, Tom hunted down the original owner's name. You were looking for records in the daughter's married name. The farm was called the Zeiss farm for so long that no one remembered Mr. Kasten established it.

Auntie Heather nods. "You're right. We never thought of that. Excellent work."

"Couldn't the original will be cross referenced with her name, anyway?" Packmom asks.

I am a brilliant basset hound, but this makes no sense to me. I'd rather take a nap, but Karly is too excited and it's traveling right down the leash. Sigh. I stand up and shake off. I need to potty. I need to stay and listen.

Decisions, decisions.

If I stay, I'll have to squat. There isn't even a clump of grass to mark. I can only move a little bit away. Karly's leash is irritating. Now that we are fully bonded, I can find her anywhere. She doesn't need it.

I squat. How embarrassing.

Peeing like a puppy. It's also a waste of good marking material, too. At least I'm not missing anything. A stream puddles beneath me and my paws get a little wet. I step back to Karly's side.

"Ick. Seriously, you couldn't hold it?"

Hey, I'm a dog. You wanted me to wait for a bathroom?

"That's where Tom comes in. A few years ago the county records office computerized all the files. Before that, everything was put on microfilm, He thinks the will wasn't transferred to either microfilm or the computer."

Yup. More technowhatsit failure. Too much relying on writing things down.

"There is nothing wrong with our memories, George. People just need more proof. We live much longer."

As if I didn't know that. I find the whole idea of owning land puzzling. What's the point? Power places are for everyone.

Packmom looks between me and Auntie Heather. She shakes her head slowly. "We can do something, then. We can search the microfilm, or the original papers."

Packdad groans. "That's where things get sticky. We know roughly when the will was filed, but Tom already looked. Most of the microfilms were destroyed when they were transferred to computer. They weren't in the greatest of shape. He did find out that some of the older records were sent to the library for their historical value. Unfortunately, the last time he went to look through old records everything was out of order."

Packmom grins. "Is everyone's library card up to date?"

What's a library card?

Chapter Twenty-Four

I am sitting outside the library holding Joey's leash. He keeps running around shrieking. I think he's happy. I'm not. What are they doing in there? I try to find a comfortable spot to nap, but Joey keeps jerking my neck. This Boypup needs basic classes in obedience.

The door to the library swings out and Karly bounces to me, taking her leash from Joey. Thank goodness. I take a deep breath.

Phew. It's nice to have a well-trained Peep.

"We found it! The will! We found it! The last box! It was in the last box, squished on the bottom." She picks up my front paws and dances with me. I am *not* built for dancing. She's too excited to pick up my discomfort through our link. I try to push away. That doesn't work. I nudge her hands with my nose.

"Sorry George." She lowers me back to the ground. Finally. Two feet aren't as stable as four. "My history teacher found the will! Don't you get it? The woods are safe! The Hodag will go away. The woods are ours again! It can't be turned into a subdivision!"

I still don't understand how Peeps can own the land, but whatever. The Horrible Hodag is going away. Arrrrooooo! Yes! The woods are safe! Joey is safe.

The Boypup is strangely quiet. If he wasn't standing and breathing I'd think he's dead. The walking dead, since he's moved to Karly's side and is pulling at her shirt.

"No! She can't go. She's my best forever friend." He starts to cry. "Tell me she's not going to leave."

Karly pats him. I sit on his foot. It's to keep him from doing anything stupid. He could run back to the woods and try to find The Horrible Hodag. My eyes widen. What if he tries to go with her? Hmmm. My Girlpup gives me a not-nice look. Okay, yeah, the Packfamily wouldn't be happy. I lean into him. Petting me will make him feel better.

He moves away and sits on a bench next to the building in a little garden. Karly and I follow him. She sits next to him. I hike my leg on the bench leg.

Mine.

The Packpups slide away and Karly looks around and moans.

"At least no one was watching," she murmurs.

Boypup is still crying when the rest of the Pack comes out of the library. I wonder what's in there. I smell books. There must be something else. Maybe computers like Karly's. I'm glad I'm outside where I don't have to curl up under the desk. Boring.

My Pack sees Joey crying and comes over. Packdad tilts the Boypup's head back with a finger under his chin. "What's wrong?"

Joey sniffles and tries to talk through his crying. "You…" Sniff. "Are…" Sniff. "Making…" Sniff. "Her go away." Sniff. "She's the only one that likes me," he wails.

"That's not true. You have a lot of friends. Justin, Scott, Jared," Packdad tells him.

I woofle.

Packdad grins. "George."

"He isn't my friend." He points to Karly. "George is hers."

Can't argue with the Boypup. Except, for the "hers" part. Everyone knows she's mine.

Auntie Heather is whispering with Packmom. Packmom nods her head. Wonder what that's all about?

Chapter Twenty-Five

We are eating in the picnic area of the park. I raise my snout from my supper dish. It's filled with all sorts of nummies. Mainly green beans, but there are bits of chicken, tomatoes, and hamburger. It seems all so normal.

The Hodag must've known her woods are safe because she's not there anymore. Even her trash heap is gone. Most of the trash in the park is gone. The animals are back and making happy noises. The mosquitoes bite, the birds sing, the squirrels are obnoxious, and the rabbits...rabbit? Rabbitrabbitrabbit!

Where? There is the slightest whiff of one coming from the field. I feel Karly staring at me. She puts a carrot cupcake into my bowl. "I didn't forget you."

I inhale the cupcake with one gulp.

More? Yup, one piece. I snag the last bit of hamburger. Swallow it. I plunge into the bowl, sucking in all the numminess and lick it clean.

Karly removes the leash from the post where she hooked the handle and releases me from the other end. Why can't she unsnap the thing and take it with her? Why does she even need it anymore, she's fine now without it.

Karly plops on the ground next to me, crosses her legs and props her elbows on her knees. She blows out her breath and her hair puffs away from her face. It's easier to watch everyone without hair in the way. She needs grooming. My fur is a perfect length. I give my leg a swipe with my tongue. Karly strokes my back. I arch into it.

More.

I stick my nose in Karly's neck.

She smell/tastes of Girl/pup/soap/smoke/burger. With an undernote of...the good soap Auntie Heather makes. No chemicals. She smiles.

My Girlpup is smell/tasting through me. I lick her and she giggles.

"Auntie Heather is showing me how to make stuff so I don't sweat and stink up the place. What I think stinks—not what you think does. I won't get embarrassed around friends. You won't get sick."

Compromise. The Girlpup is growing up. Sure takes long enough with Peeps.

Oh. My tummy isn't happy. I check to see if there is anything left in my dish. Nothing.

Tummy still feels bad—grass'll fix it. I amble over and snarf down a little.

Still not quite right.

I hork up what is bothering me. Karly makes her own horking noise. She doesn't make the sound right at all, but what do Peeps know about such important matters?

Hmmm. There isn't anything in the pile that should bother me. I gobble it back up. Yep, that's better. Actually, it tastes better the second time around.

Karly is edging away from me. Uh-uh. Tell me how everything worked out.

"Ick. George, that was gross. How could you do that?"

That is the dumbest question the Girlpup has ever asked me. I roll my eyes. Hey. How did the Hodag know she could go? I know she can understand me now.

She shrugs. "I'm not sure. Dad said that the developers weren't happy, but they came and got their trucks and stuff. Maybe she saw them go."

Auntie Heather walks up, eyes the spot where I had seconds of my dinner, and shakes her head.

"Is your stomach upset, or did you eat too fast?"

I wag my tail. My tummy is just fine.

"Did you see the woods? Every single can, candy wrapper, and bag is gone. I don't think she cleaned up the park on purpose—she loves her shiny things. It's a shame we don't know where she went. Or where the animals were." Auntie Heather shrugs. "I didn't realize how much more magic there was in those books. It'll keep us busy."

My super hearing picks up Joey crying to his mom, who is sitting at a picnic table.

"Bu…bu…but, she was my friend. Why didn't she tell me she was going?"

I want to ignore him, but I smell something interesting.

It isn't Packmom, who is wiping his tears and snot from his face with the hem of her shirt. I'd do it with my tongue. What do I smell?

"Honey, she had to go back to her house. I'm sure she's sad she couldn't say good-bye to you. Look, Auntie Heather has something for you that'll make you happy. Why don't you go see what it is?"

Boypup springs off Packmom's lap and over to Auntie Heather. He's loyal like that.

Snort.

Boypups.

Now, what *is* that I smell/taste? It's familiar.

"Bark, bark, bark."

The soprano sound hits my ears before I see her pulling to Joey. Patches of tan and white, long, small wriggly body, short legs, long ears.

She's beautiful.

"Auntie Heather! Is she mine? Mom! Can I keep her? Puhleeze?"

A puppygirl basset.

Oh, yeah! "Aroooooo". Can we keep her? I can already tell she's going to grow up to be a looker.

Not sure what I think about Joey raising her. With Karly and me on the job, he shouldn't be able to wreck her. I strain against the leash, introduce me already.

Auntie Heather hands the leash to Joey. The little puppygirl is cute. Her paws are too big and she trips over her ears. I think I'm in love. Come on Karly, I want to meet her.

"Her name is Tillie. Be very careful with her, she's only three months old." Auntie Heather smiles at the Boypup and the puppygirl.

"Is she really mine? Mom?" Joey pleads with "basset eyes." He's been practicing.

Yeah, is she really ours? I slip out of my collar and amble over.

Well, hello there Tillie. What's up?

Apparently her belly as she roles over to establish who's alpha. I am in love. I sniff her butt, nuzzle her belly, and lick in her ears. She smell/tastes of newsprintpuppychowmilk. One of my favorite smell/tastes.

"The way you made friends with the Hodag showed your dad and me that you were ready for your own puppy. You're in charge of feeding, cleaning, and training her, though. She's just a baby and you don't want to get her in trouble or hurt, right? Can you handle that?"

If he can't, I will. Except the feeding part—no way is she getting my food.

Food? I walk over to my supper dish.

It's empty.

Sigh.

About the Author

Mindy Mymudes runs with the Muddy Paws Pack in Milwaukee, WI. She insists she is alpha, even as the dogs walk all over her. She hunts, cleans the den and keeps them entertained. When she can escape the pack, she enjoys digging in dirt, listening to audiobooks, and weaving the antics of the pack into stories. The alpha male, Tall Dude, just shakes his head and stays out of the way.

* * * *

Did you enjoy George Knows? If so, please help us spread the word about Mindy Mymudes and MuseItUp Publishing. It's as easy as:

•Recommend the book to your family and friends
•Post a review
•Tweet and Facebook about it

Thank you
MuseItUp Publishing

MuseItUp Publishing
Where Muse authors entertain readers!
https://museituppublishing.com
Visit our website for more books for your reading pleasure.

You can also find us on Facebook:
http://www.facebook.com/MuseItUp
and on Twitter:
http://twitter.com/MusePublishing

CPSIA information can be obtained at www.ICGtesting.com
Printed in the USA
LVOW08s1113290514

387767LV00001B/163/P